THE TRUTH ABOUT EDDIE JAMES

JESSICA R. GLASPIE

GLASPIE
PUBLICATIONS

This novel is a work of fiction. Names, descriptions, entities, and incidents included in the story are products of the author's imagination. Any resemblance to actual persons, events, and entities is entirely coincidental.

Printed in The United States of America

Cover design by Rebecca Pau

ISBN: 0-9992045-0-5

ISBN- 13: 987-0-9992045-0-4

Women's Fiction

For the victims,
Your life is the only thing that truly belongs to you. Do not give anyone the power to take it. May your desire to live be stronger than the fear.

For the survivors,
Keep encouraging more victims to survive. May you have the strength to continue your healing and the endurance to keep moving forward.

CONTENTS

1

It was about two in the afternoon on a humid day in early August when Alex drove into the parking lot of the Gatesville Shopping Center. She pulled into a parking space in front of one of the stores and hopped out of the car. *I can't believe I forgot those storage containers,* she thought to herself as she walked toward the Home section of the store. She turned onto the aisle with the containers and walked up to a large one and pulled it down.

"Can I help you with that?" a voice said behind her.

"No, thanks," Alex said, not looking back, "I've got it."

"Are you sure?" the voice came again, "I don't mind helping you. Especially someone as beautiful as you are."

Alex pulled down a second container and put it on top of the first. Then she turned around to see who was speaking to her. She saw an attractive man smiling and staring back at her. He had a gorgeous smile and dark brown eyes. Alex stared into them trying not to get lost. He looked like he was at least six feet tall and he was wearing a shirt that was showing off his muscular arms.

"No, thank you, I've got it," Alex said, smiling back at him. She turned back around to grab a third container. When she turned around to place the third container on top of the others, she noticed that the man was still standing there. "I'm sorry. Am I in your way?" Alex asked.

"No, not at all. I'm just admiring the view," he said.

"Excuse me?" Alex said frowning.

"Please don't take that the wrong way. I just happen to think that you are a very attractive woman."

"Thank you," Alex said timidly.

"You're welcome. So what's your name?" he asked, leaning against a shelf.

"Alexandria, but you can call me Alex."

"Does Alex have a last name?" he said jokingly.

"Stamford."

"Well, it's nice to meet you, Alex Stamford. My name is Edward James, but you may call me Eddie." He extended his right hand toward her. Alex grabbed it and shook it. His grip was strong and confident.

"It's nice to meet you, Eddie."

"I'm sure it is,"Eddie said as he winked at Alex. "So are you sure you don't need help with those containers? I really don't mind." Alex looked at Eddie for a moment. She knew she could carry the containers by herself, but Eddie was incredibly persistent.

"What could it hurt?" Alex said, shrugging to appear indifferent.

Eddie walked over to the containers and bent over to pick them up. Alex could smell his cologne in the air. "Are these all you're getting?"

"What?" Alex said, still taking in the aroma of the cologne. "Do you need to get anything else or are you going to the register?" he asked smiling.

"No, that's it," Alex said, coming back to reality. She hoped that Eddie wasn't watching her. She felt embarrassed.

"Okay, then I will walk you up there."

"But you don't have anything. Did you need to get something?"

"Just superglue and socks."

"Oh. I can grab them for you on the way to the register since you are carrying my containers."

"Thanks, Alex. That would be nice." Alex and Eddie began to walk toward the register. When they passed by the men's section, she grabbed the socks that Eddie wanted. During the walk, Alex couldn't help staring at Eddie. She made up in her mind that he was the most attractive man that she had ever seen. He seemed so confident and charming. He had an incredible body from what she could see, and the smell of his cologne was intoxicating. Every time he smiled, she felt her heart flutter and looking into his eyes made her knees go weak. Alex couldn't believe that he was actually interested in her.

When they got to the register, Eddie put the storage containers on the conveyor belt and grabbed a pack of superglue and put it on as well. Alex put the socks on the belt. The cashier began to scan the storage containers. When she finished, she picked up the socks and scanned them. "Oh, no! I'm sorry," Alex said to the cashier, "we aren't together."

"Not yet," Eddie said smiling. Alex blushed and smiled. "I meant the containers and your stuff, Eddie."

"Well, why not," he said, pulling out his wallet. "Ring up the glue, too. I'll pay for it."

"No, I can't let you do that, Eddie."

"Well, I'm doing it." Eddie pulled a credit card out of his wallet and swiped it in the credit card machine.

"Eddie—"

"It's too late, Alex. It's paid for."

"I really can't let you do that, Eddie. Let me give you your money back." Alex reached into her back pocket and pulled out some cash.

"I don't want your money, Alex."

"Well, I don't feel comfortable with you paying for my containers so whether you want the money or not, you're going to get it back."

Eddie looked at Alex for a second. Then he smiled at her. "Sassy. I like it. I'll tell you what. Go to dinner with me on Friday and we will call it even."

"Okay, but only if you let me pay."

"I can consider it. Now come on, let me walk you to your car." Eddie smiled at Alex and picked up the storage containers. She grabbed his bag from the bag carousel and they began to walk toward the exit. "So where is your car?"

"Right there," Alex said, pointing to a Honda Accord in the row directly in front of them. They walked up to the car and Alex popped the trunk. Eddie put two of the containers into the trunk and one on the backseat. When he closed the door, he looked at Alex and she handed him his bag.

"So when is a good time to call you, Alex?"

"You don't even have my number, Eddie."

"I know, but I figured you were going to give it to me since you agreed to have dinner with me." Alex smiled and gave Eddie her phone number. "Thank you. Can I call you tonight?"

"Sure."

"Great. Talk to you later, Alex," Eddie said, winking, before turning to walk away.

"See you, Eddie." Alex opened her door and got into the car. She sat behind the wheel for a moment and watched Eddie walk across the parking lot. She couldn't believe she had a date with him. She was elated. Alex backed out of the parking space and drove out of the parking lot. She couldn't wait to get home and tell her mom all about Eddie James.

2

*A*lex turned off the water from her shower and grabbed her towel from the drying rack. It was late Friday afternoon and Alex was preparing for her date with Eddie. She walked out of the bathroom and went into her room. She couldn't believe the day was finally here. Eddie turned out to be just as charming and sweet over the phone as he had been the day they met. They talked on the phone for hours at a time, and every day, she found herself liking Eddie more and more.

He was extremely well spoken and had an amazing sense of humor. He seemed so down to earth. Alex opened the sliding doors to her closet and stood there looking at the clothes. She had no idea what she was going to wear. She wanted to look nice for Eddie. She took a blue dress, a red skirt, and a black blouse out of her closet and laid them on the bed.

"Knock, knock," came her mother's voice from the doorway.

"Hey, Mom. What's up?"

"So tonight is your big date?" she asked, walking in and sitting on Alex's bed.

"Yea, and I'm really looking forward to it."

"What are you going to wear?"

"I can't decide between the blue dress and the red and black outfit."

"Well, you look beautiful in both."

"Thanks, Mom, but that doesn't help."

"Wear the blue."

"Thanks."

"Where is he taking you?"

"I'm not sure actually. He said he wanted to surprise me."

"Well, that's nice."

"Yea, it is. It seems like he put a lot of thought into our date," Alex grinned.

"So tell me about this guy, Alex. What do you know about him?"

"I actually know a lot about him. We've talked every day since we met."

"Okay, then tell me about him."

Alex studied her mother's face in search of a motive behind all of her questions. Her facial expression looked innocent enough so Alex said, "I've already told you about him. What else would you like to know?"

"I want to know general information. Like, how old he is, what he does for a living, things of that nature. All you really told me about him is he's cute, and you think you like him."

"Okay. Well, his name is Edward Steven James and he is gorgeous."

"Yes, we've established that. Go on."

"He is eighteen years old, like me, and he is a student. He is smart, funny, and charming. I could really see a future with him."

Her mother frowned. "You just met him, Alex."

"I know that."

"Well, do you really think it's wise to be so into a guy you just met? And what will happen when you leave in a couple of weeks for college? Do you think it's wise to start some kind of relationship when you're about to leave?"

"He's leaving too. Coincidentally, we're both enrolled in Pendleton University. We will be there together, so we wouldn't have to worry about anything long distance."

"I see." Alex's mother sighed and crossed her legs. "Alex," she began slowly, "I see that you are really interested in this guy, but I wouldn't be doing my job as your mother if I didn't give you some advice."

"What's that?" Alex said, rolling her eyes. She knew the "mom speech" was coming.

"Be very careful as to what you decide to place at the top of your priority list."

"What does that mean?"

"It means I am not paying for you to go to college so you can find a husband. You are going for an education and to make something of yourself."

"I know that, Mom."

"Going off to college is a big transition, Alex. It is so much easier to make that transition if you aren't splitting your attention between your studies and a boy."

"I got it, Mom," Alex said a little more harshly than she meant to. Her mom seemed to see Alex's defenses go up, so she fell silent for a moment. She knew her mother meant well, but Alex wished she would back off sometimes. She had done more than enough in her life to prove that she was capable of making responsible decisions. Alex knew that she had her priorities in order. She wasn't going to let anyone, especially Eddie, stop her from accomplishing her goal of becoming a high school counselor.

"I love you, Alex," her mom began again, "and I only want you to make good decisions. You're my baby. You're all I have left and I want you to excel. Just think about what I've said, okay?"

Alex looked at her mother as she cried silently. She walked over to her mother and sat beside her. She gave her a hug and wiped the tears from her mother's eyes. Alex knew all too well why her mother was crying. Alex's father and older brother, Brian, died in a tragic car accident when she was fourteen. She remembered that day as if it just happened.

It had rained all day and the roads were a mess. That morning, her father and brother were talking about the professional basketball game they were going to that night. They were challenging each other on who could make the most creative paper ball shots into the wastebasket from across the kitchen. Alex's mother was fussing at them for wasting paper and trying to hurry them out of the door for school and work. They grabbed their bags and prepared to leave. Alex's father grabbed her mother and gave her a long lingering kiss good-bye.

He looked into her eyes and said, "I love you, Michaela." Then he let go and walked over to Alex to give her a kiss on the cheek. "Bye, babe," he said to her before walking out of the door toward his car. Brian put his bag on his back and grabbed Alex from behind and put her in a headlock. "Love you, squirt!" he said, kissing her on the head. Alex remembered pushing him away and saying, "yea, yea" and smiling. She remembered him saying "love you, Mom" to their mother before running out of the door. That was the last time Alex saw them alive.

Even though Alex and Brian went to the same school, they wouldn't see each other during the day because of their conflicting schedules. After school, she went to dance class and he went to basketball practice. That day, her mother picked her up from her dance class and her father picked up her brother from practice. They were going to travel to the game after Brian's practice. When the game was over, they called the house to tell Alex and her mother that they were on their way home. They sounded so excited about the outcome of the game.

At about two in the morning, Alex's mother was frantic. She didn't know where her husband or son would be at that hour. She told Alex that she was going to drive on the road that they would have taken to see if maybe something bad had happened to them. Alex wanted to ride with her, but her mom wouldn't let her.

Around six in the morning, Alex's grandfather came to get Alex and take her to the hospital. When she got there, she saw her mother sitting in a chair with a nurse on both sides of her, and she was shaking. Her mother seemed distant and she didn't look at Alex. She just stared into space with tears streaming down her face. Alex could only assume the worst; her father and brother were dead. She began to feel lightheaded and her knees buckled. Her grandfather helped her to a chair. Alex remembered that her grandfather sat beside her and told her what happened.

He told her that when her mother found the totaled car, the police were already at the scene. Due to the slippery road conditions, her father's car hit a standing puddle of water and slid to the other side of the road where they had a head on collision with a tractor-trailer. The collision would have killed them instantly; the police said they didn't suffer. The accident was so bad that they had to get the Jaws of Life to pull apart the car. The bodies were so crushed that they weren't recognizable. Alex's mother identified the bodies by her husband's wedding ring.

Alex wiped the tears from her own eyes and stood up again. She walked over to her closet and took out the pair of blue espadrilles that matched her dress and placed them on the floor beside her bed.

"I know that it has to be hard for you to see me leave, Mom."

"It is," her mom said, wiping tears from her cheeks, "but I

know you make good decisions. You have a good head on your shoulders and I'm proud of you."

"Thanks, Mom, Alex smiled."

"Well, I am going to let you finish getting ready."

Alex's mom stood up and walked over to Alex and gave her a hug. When she walked out of the room, Alex picked up the red skirt and black blouse and put them back in the closet. Then she went and sat beside her blue dress on the bed. She felt so bad for her mom sometimes. Her mom never remarried and she barely dated. It almost seemed like after her husband died, she decided to die with him. It made Alex's heart heavy just thinking about it. She decided that it was time to think about something else. Eddie.

She began to wonder where he was going to take her. He wouldn't even give her a hint. All he said was that he had a plan and she would love it. Alex wasn't the biggest fan of surprises, but she decided to put her feelings aside and be open to this date. She put on her clothes and walked into the bathroom. As she plugged in her curling iron, she couldn't help but think about her conversations with Eddie.

They seemed to have so much in common. They both graduated within the top 5 percent of their high school classes and they both worked at a fast food restaurant during high school. They seemed to have the same hobbies and they liked the same music. Whenever they talked, it seemed like they knew each other for years.

Eddie was a dream and Alex was beginning to wonder if he was just too good to be true. Most women would kill for a man like him. He was tall and attractive. He was confident, charming, and funny. He was so intelligent and seemed to appreciate the beauty in life. Alex picked up the curling iron and began to curl her hair. *What an amazing man,* she thought.

Alex was about halfway through her hair when she heard the

doorbell. She peeked into her bedroom to look at her alarm clock. It read 6:30p.m. *That couldn't be Eddie, could it?* she wondered. If it was, Alex knew she had another thirty minutes to go before she would be ready. Alex walked back in the bathroom and closed the door. She heard her mom walk to the door and open it.

"Hello, Mrs. Stamford," Alex heard Eddie say. "My name is Eddie James. I am here to pick up Alex for our date."

"Hello, Eddie, it's nice to meet you. Come in please. Alex isn't ready yet. She said she wasn't expecting you until 7:00 p.m." Alex heard the door close.

"Yes, ma'am, I know. But I wanted to come by early so that you could meet me and see who your daughter is going out with."

"Isn't that considerate? Thank you, Eddie."

"By the way, these are for you." Alex heard a rustle of paper. She assumed that Eddie brought her mother flowers.

"Aren't you sweet? Thank you. I'll go and put these in some water. Have a seat in the living room, and I will join you in a few." Alex heard Eddie walk into the living room, and she heard her mother moving around in the kitchen. She had to be dreaming. Alex never dated a guy who came to her house early just to speak to her mother, let alone bring her mother flowers. Eddie James seemed like he was the real deal.

Butterflies fluttered in her stomach with the rising anticipation of going on the date. Alex had never met anyone who was such a gentleman. As she continued to curl her hair, she moved closer to the door to listen to the conversation between her mother and Eddie. All she could hear were pieces of phrases. She wasn't worried about Eddie saying anything rude or her mother getting too personal with Eddie, so she decided to stop eavesdropping.

When Alex was almost finished with her hair, she heard a loud laugh. It was her mother laughing. It startled Alex so much that she dropped the curling iron on the floor. She hadn't heard her mother laugh like that since before her father and brother died. It was refreshing to hear. Alex quickly picked up the curling iron and put it on the counter. She couldn't believe that Eddie got her mom to laugh like that. She had only gotten her mother to smile and lightly chuckle. She wondered what Eddie said to her to make her laugh like she did. Alex finished her hair and walked out of the bathroom.

"Hey, babe, you coming out?" Alex heard her mom calling to her.

"Not yet," Alex said.

She walked into her room and finished getting ready. When she reached the living room, she saw Eddie sitting beside her mother, who was holding the family photo album.

"Hi, Eddie," Alex said smiling.

She couldn't believe how good he looked. He was wearing a short sleeve, red and white striped polo shirt with blue jeans and white shoes. He wore a watch on his left wrist and he looked as if he had a fresh haircut.

He smiled at Alex and said, "Hey, Alex. You look beautiful. These are for you." He reached beside him and picked up a bouquet of roses. Then he stood up and extended them to her. Alex put her purse down on the couch and took the flowers.

"Thank you, Eddie."

"Well, don't you look lovely? Go put those in some water, babe, and we will finish looking at the album," Alex's mother said. Eddie sat back down beside her and Alex walked into the kitchen. Eddie had done it again; what a charmer. Alex was impressed that he was doing so well with her mother. She found a vase in one of the cabinets, filled it with water, and placed the flowers in it. She could hear her mother telling stories about Alex when she was a little girl; she sounded so happy. When she walked out of the kitchen, her mother was just closing the photo album.

"Are you ready to go?" Alex asked Eddie.

"Yes, I am," Eddie said standing. "It was nice meeting you, Mrs. Stamford. I had a great time looking at your photo album."

"Anytime, Eddie. It was nice meeting you, too. And please just call me Ms. Michaela," Alex's mother said, rising from the couch as well. "You two have a good time and drive safely."

"Okay, Ms. Michaela. I will."

Eddie reached over and gave Alex's mom a quick hug.

Then Alex embraced her mother. "I love you, Mom," she said.

"I love you too, babe." Her mother walked into the kitchen, and Eddie and Alex walked toward the door.

3

"So where are we going?" Alex asked as they headed to Eddie's car.

"It's a surprise," Eddie said, looking at Alex and smiling. "You look incredible in that dress, if I do say so myself."

"Thank you. It's one of my favorites."

Eddie walked over to the passenger side door and opened it for Alex. The car smelled fresh like it had just been detailed. Eddie got into the driver's side and closed the door. His cologne immediately filled the air.

"This is a nice car, Eddie. Is it yours?" Alex asked, admiring the interior of the car.

"No, it's my dad's. He let me borrow it for this date."

"To make a good impression?"

"Yea, something like that." Eddie glanced at Alex and smiled.

She smiled shyly back. "So what kind of car is this?"

"A Porsche."

"Oh, okay. I've heard good things about Porsches."

"Yea, they're good cars."

"Your father must be very good at what he does."

"He is. He's a lawyer, a partner in his own firm. They handle a lot of high profile cases."

"What kind of law does he practice?"

"Criminal."

"Oh, is that the same kind that you want to practice?"

"It is."

"Well, that's wonderful that you want to follow in your father's footsteps."

"Yea. I believe it's important for me to follow his example. He is a great man, a terrific father, and an excellent provider. I can't think of a better role model."

"I bet." Alex turned and looked out of the window. The discussion about Eddie's father made her think of her own. He was a wonderful man, too. He was an accountant who was quickly climbing the ranks at his firm. Alex used to tease him about his love for numbers. He would always say, "One plus one will always equal two" and that used to excite him for reasons she never understood. He loved the consistency and the predictability of numbers. Alex let out a sigh. She really missed him.

"You okay, Alex?"

Alex turned forward again. "Yea, why do you ask?"

"You got quiet on me."

"Yea. Just thinking."

"About what?"

"About where you could be taking me for our date," Alex said smiling. She didn't want to tell Eddie what she was really thinking about. She mentioned to Eddie during their phone conversations that her father and brother passed away, but she hadn't gone into detail. She made up in her mind that she would tell him later, but she knew that a first date was not the place to bring up such a heavy topic.

"You'll see," Eddie said smiling. "We're almost there."

"Okay. So let me ask you something?"

"Shoot."

"How did you get my mom to laugh like she did?"

"What do you mean?"

"When I was doing my hair, I heard her laughing. What were you two talking about?"

"She was telling me about the first time your father decided he wanted to make a pizza."

"Oh, yea! I remember that," Alex laughed. "He kept toss- ing the dough in the air until it got stuck on the ceiling. He stayed in the kitchen for hours waiting for it to fall down, but it didn't. Then at about three in the morning, he went to get some water and the dough fell on his head and startled him. After that inci- dent, he swore he would never make anything with dough in it again."

"He didn't really mean that, did he?"

"No. He was right back in the kitchen trying to make another pizza a few days later. He was the kind of person who never quit."

"Sounds like a pretty determined guy."

"Yea, he was. I'd almost forgotten about that."

Alex became silent again. It was a memory of Alex's father that made her mother laugh like she did, not something Eddie said. Knowing that made Alex's heart feel good. She always knew she would celebrate the day when her mom could reminisce about her father without crying. She wasn't optimistic when her mom cried over the memory of the accident earlier that day. But her laughter about the pizza incident had to be some sign of progress.

About five minutes later, Eddie drove into the parking lot at Nelson's Glow in the Dark Mini-Golf Arena. "Okay, we're here," he said.

"So this is the big surprise? Glow in the dark mini-golf?" "One of many. The night is just getting started. Are you ready?"

"Sure."

Eddie and Alex got out of the car. They walked into the mini-golf arena and Alex's eyes lit up with all the fluorescent colors in the place. She couldn't wait to try this. Eddie was right; she was truly surprised. Eddie handed her a golf ball and a club, and they walked to the first hole.

"How about we make this interesting," Eddie said.

"How so?"

"Let's make a bet."

"What kind of bet?"

"Like, if I win, I get a kiss by the end of the date." Alex stared at Eddie through the darkness. His teeth were even brighter than normal due to the special lighting in the arena.

"And if I win?" Alex asked.

"Tell me what you want and I will give it to you."

Alex thought about it for a moment. "I want to know about the rest of the date."

Eddie looked at Alex. "That's all you want?"

"Yea."

"Wow, I'm shocked."

"Why?"

"Because I expected you to ask for something material. You know, like a new outfit, shoes, jewelry. Something like that."

"Who does that?" Alex smirked.

"You'd be surprised, Alex. When women find out you have money, they try to get what they can from you."

"How would a woman know you have money unless you tell them?"

"My dad's car."

"Oh. So they see you drive up in that car and see that you might have access to some money and start drooling over it."

"Pretty much. So I use my dad's car as a test. If a female seems like she's into the car more than she's into me, she's not the one and she shouldn't expect a second date."

"And what about the bet?"

"Ah, the nail in the coffin. I ask for a bet, they agree. When she asks for something material, I find an excuse to take her home."

"Wow, that's pretty serious."

"Yea, it is. I want a woman who wants me for me, not for what she thinks I can buy her."

"Makes sense."

"It does, doesn't it?"

"So did I pass?"

"With flying colors. I'm very impressed."

"Thank you."

"All right. I win, I get a kiss. You win, I tell you about the rest of the date."

"I thought the bet was just a test."

"It was until you passed. But I'd be lying if I said I didn't want that kiss." Alex could see Eddie smiling, so she smiled back.

"Let's just play, Eddie."

"No bet?"

"Let's see how the night goes."

"Fair enough."

Alex knew that she wanted to kiss Eddie. It had been on her mind all day. She kept imagining what it might be like. She hoped he was a good kisser because if the date went well, she was definitely going to kiss him. Alex teed off first and then Eddie. They went through all of the holes fairly quickly. They were laughing and flirting throughout the entire game. When the game was over, they returned their clubs and walked out of the arena.

When they got in the car, Eddie said, "Next stop." He backed out of the parking space and proceeded to drive out of the shopping center. Alex didn't have to wait long for the next surprise.

Eddie took her to a restaurant about five minutes from the mini-golf arena.

"We're here," Eddie said smiling. He really seemed to be relishing the fact that he was surprising Alex at every turn. They got out of the car and Alex surveyed the building. She recognized this restaurant. It was called Paulette's and she had been dying to go since it opened five years ago. She would often ride past it with her mom and wonder what it was like inside. Alex couldn't believe that she was finally going to eat there. Eddie opened the door to the restaurant for Alex and they walked in.

"Welcome to Paulette's!" the hostess said with a warm smile. "What is your last name?"

"James," Eddie said.

"Oh," said the hostess looking flustered and smiling shyly. "Please wait here."

She walked away and disappeared behind a door in the back of the restaurant. When she came back, she was led by a thin, older woman with big brown eyes and long flowing hair. She extended her arms toward Eddie.

"Eddie! How are you, Honey?" she asked in a surprisingly deep voice that didn't match her small frame.

"I'm fine, Aunt Paulette. How are you?" Eddie asked hugging her.

"I can't complain, Sweetheart. I'm so glad you're here. I was so excited when you said you wanted to bring a date here. Hi, you must be Alex!" she said, directing her attention toward Alex. "It's wonderful to meet you." She reached out and hugged Alex.

"It is nice to meet you too, Mrs. Paulette," Alex said.

"Have you ever been here before, Honey?" Paulette grinned.

"No ma'am, but I've heard wonderful things about your restaurant."

"Good! Then I know you won't be disappointed," Paulette winked. "Come with me."

Paulette grabbed two menus and started walking toward the center of the restaurant. She stopped at a table with a reserved sign on it and laid the menus in front of the two chairs. Eddie and Alex sat down and opened their menus.

"Your server will be with you shortly. Order anything you want and if you need me, you know where to find me."

Paulette winked at Alex and lovingly squeezed Eddie's shoulder before she walked back through the door from which she emerged. Alex didn't even know where to begin. What were the odds that Eddie knew the owner of the restaurant that she had always wanted to go to? Since she couldn't find the words to speak, Alex just looked around the restaurant in awe.

"So you've never been here before?" Eddie asked, bringing Alex out of her daze.

"No, I haven't. I've always wanted to, though. Thanks for bringing me here," Alex said, trying not to appear too impressed.

"No problem. I know you'll love it. Paulette's recipes are incredible."

"Don't you mean *Aunt Paulette?*"

"Yea, I guess. She actually isn't my real aunt. She is just so close to my family that she is like a sister to my parents. So I call her Aunt Paulette. She's a really sweet lady. She's been really good to me and my family."

"It's good that you have such a strong family unit."

Eddie nodded. "So tell me, what're you thinking about getting?" he asked.

"I'm not sure. The linguine with clams sounds good, but then again so does the steak and lobster."

"Steak and lobster? Wow, you have a healthy appetite, don't you?"

"Yea. I'm not one of those girls who refuses to eat because she is trying to watch her weight. When I'm hungry, I eat."

"That is so refreshing to hear. Order whatever you want, Alex. It's on me."

"No, it isn't."

Eddie put down his menu and stared at Alex from across the table. "Why is that?"

"I agreed to go out with you if I could pay for the meal."

"The meal is going to be a lot more than the storage containers, Alex."

"I realize that. But it is important for me to be a woman of my word."

"Look, Alex, I'm sure you are a woman of your word, but I can't in good conscience let you pay for this meal. Can we just say you owe me one?"

Alex put her menu down and stared at Eddie. It bothered her that she couldn't pay Eddie back for the storage containers. She was too independent to allow him to pay without her giving him his money back. But she also knew that she could not afford to pay for the meal. Alex put her pride aside and agreed that Eddie should pay for the meal. They both picked their menus back up and stared at them until the server came.

When he came, he introduced himself as "Mitch" and took their drink and meal orders. He brought bread to the table and Eddie took a piece off the plate. Alex studied Eddie as he ate the bread. She wasn't sure why Eddie wouldn't allow her to pay him back for the storage containers. She hoped that Eddie's resistance to accepting her money was not geared by chauvinist motives, because if he had a problem with women paying for things, they would have a serious problem.

Alex was not the type of woman who wanted to sit back and be taken care of by a man. She shook her head. It wouldn't be wise to jump to conclusions, especially since their first date wasn't even over yet. Plus, he seemed like a nice guy. Alex told herself that he was just being a gentleman and wanted to make a good first impression.

After about twenty minutes, the server brought out their food and they ate. They talked about leaving home for the first time and finally feeling like adults. Eddie seemed so excited to leave home, but Alex was a little hesitant. She had never been away from her mother for an extended period of time before, and she was worried about how her mother would handle an empty nest. Alex planned on encouraging her to get out of the house more and live life.

When they were done eating, the server came back to collect the plates.

"Are you interested in trying one of our desserts tonight?" Mitch asked after the table was cleared.

"Yes," Eddie said.

"Oh no, Eddie. I can't eat another bite."

"Well, I would like dessert, Mitch," Eddie said, looking at Mitch.

"Yes, sir, I will bring you the dessert menu."

"No need, Mitch. I know what I want. Bring me a slice of Paulette's famous chocolate mousse cake. You sure you don't want dessert, Alex?" Eddie asked, staring intently at her. "You could always eat it later."

Alex had heard incredible things about Paulette's chocolate mousse cake. She would have loved to try it, but she was too full to even consider it.

"No, Eddie. I couldn't."

"I'll tell you what. I will order two slices. You can try some of mine and if you like it, you can have the second piece. If you don't, I will take it home with me."

Alex couldn't pass up an offer like that. She would like to try the cake and this way she could have the best of both worlds. She could try some of the cake without wasting it and if she liked it, she could take it home to eat when she wasn't so full.

"Okay, sounds good," she said.

"Excellent. Two please," Eddie said to Mitch. "And make them to go." Mitch walked toward the kitchen to get the cake for Eddie and Alex.

"To go? Are we going somewhere else?" Alex asked with a puzzled look on her face.

"Yes, we are."

Alex fought the urge to roll her eyes. She really wished that Eddie would just tell her where they were going. She was having a great time, but the whole "see as we go" thing was really starting to work on Alex's nerves. She forced a smile and said, "Okay."

Mitch brought two brilliantly wrapped slices of cake and the check to the table. Eddie laid a card in the money holder and sent it back with Mitch. He also put an extremely generous tip on the table. Alex just looked at him. If Eddie didn't want a female to relish the fact that he had money, he really didn't act like it. Expensive restaurant, paying for the meal without even looking at the check, and putting a large tip on the table like it was chump change; Alex assumed he was done pretending to be humble unless those were gestures to impress her. If these were gestures, she wasn't impressed.

Maybe some of the other females that Eddie dated in his past were impressed by things like that, but Alex's heart wasn't for sale. Eddie's confidence was sexy when she first met him, but now he was starting to appear arrogant. Alex only hoped that wherever they were going next would help Eddie tone it down a little.

Mitch came back with the money holder and Eddie took his card out."

"Excuse me, Mr. James," Mitch said to Eddie, "Mrs. Paulette had to take a phone call and unfortunately couldn't come see you off. She asked me to tell you good-bye."

"Thanks, Mitch," Eddie said, standing up and picking up the wrapped cake from the table.

"Oh, you're welcome, sir!" Mitch said, suddenly seeing his tip on the table.

Alex stood up as well, and she and Eddie walked outside to the car. They got in and drove out of the parking lot. He drove for about thirty minutes until Alex couldn't see streetlights any more. "Umm...Eddie? Where are we going?" Alex asked nervously.

"To your last surprise."

"My last surprise is in the middle of nowhere?"

"Yes, it is."

"Okay, you're not planning to kill me and butcher my body, are you?"

"Wow, Alex, that's kind of morbid."

"You've brought me out to the middle of nowhere on a first date. So I'm sorry if that is the first thing that came to my mind."

Eddie laughed. "You must watch a lot of crime dramas. No, Alex, I'm not going to kill you and cut up your body. I just want to end our date in a romantic, quiet place."

Alex looked out of the window of Eddie's car. All she could see were trees.

"We're here," he said, pulling onto a paved driveway that cut in between the trees. Eddie drove about half a mile on the paved driveway in the darkness. Then they reached a large clearing. Alex saw an enormous house in the clearing and there was a large pond behind the house. The house was dark and it looked as if nobody was home. Eddie pulled in front of the house and parked the car.

"Let's go," he said grinning. And bring the cake." He got out of the car and went to the trunk. Alex followed.

Oh no, Alex thought. *This is it. I'm going to die here.*

Eddie popped the trunk and Alex peered inside. Nothing suspicious. Eddie reached in and took out a blanket and a small black bag. "Follow me," he said softly. He led Alex to the back of the house and laid the blanket on the ground about twenty yards from the pond. She stood at a distance watching him, while trying to figure out what the blanket was for. She was convinced that he was going to wrap her cold, dead body in it. "Calm down," she told herself, "you're just being silly."

He extended his hand toward her. She walked slowly over to him. He took the cake from her hands and put it down beside the black bag. Eddie took both of Alex's hands in his and said, "Look, up."

Alex looked up to see the night sky full of stars. She stared at the massive expanse in awe. She had never seen the sky like that. "Wow, Eddie," Alex finally managed to say.

"It's beautiful, isn't it? I'm sorry if I scared you by bringing you out here, but I wanted this to be a real surprise. I thought we might enjoy our dessert under the stars."

Alex looked at Eddie. She didn't know what to say. This was the perfect ending to their evening. Alex was still trying to put the words together in her head, so she didn't say anything that could potentially ruin the moment. She just sat down on the blanket and handed Eddie a piece of cake. He sat down beside her and opened the cake up. He reached into his bag and pulled out two forks and handed one to Alex. She tried the cake and it was divine. She was glad that Eddie chose to get two pieces because she was definitely going to take the second piece home with her. When Eddie finished his cake, he laid back on his elbows and sighed.

"I love it out here, Alex. It's so peaceful. As soon as I could start driving, I would come out here and stare at the stars. It really helped me clear my head."

"It is absolutely lovely out here, Eddie. How did you find this place?"

"It's a family house. Everyone in the family has a key and they use it for different purposes."

"Oh, that's a good idea having a property to share. You all must have come up with a great schedule where everyone can use it equally."

"Yea, it works out well."

"I know when I was younger, my family used to go to a property like this in the mountains. It wasn't this isolated, though. It was like a neighborhood of really nice houses and they surrounded this huge lake that reflected the moon in the most beautiful way. You could never see the stars like this up there, though. I think it had something to do with the way everything was set up. But I—" Alex stopped when she realized Eddie was staring at her smiling.

"Do I have something on my face?" she asked, wiping at her face.

"No," Eddie said, sitting up and moving closer to Alex. "Not at all."

Eddie put his hand on Alex's cheek and caressed it while staring deep into her eyes. "You're beautiful. Do you know that?" Eddie asked, still staring into her eyes.

"Yes, I do," Alex said, staring back at him. She could tell by the look in his eyes that he was going to kiss her. Alex closed her eyes and leaned forward slightly. She immediately felt Eddie's lips on hers and she wanted to melt. He was a really good kisser. The kiss was everything she thought it would be. Alex pulled away and smiled shyly. Eddie looked at his watch and said, "Let's get you home before it gets too late." He packed up everything and they got back in the car. Eddie turned the car around and drove out of the driveway. He held Alex's hand the entire way back to her house. When they arrived at her house, Eddie walked her to the door.

"I would love to see you again, Alex," Eddie said when they were standing outside of Alex's front door.

"I would like that, Eddie." He leaned in and kissed Alex good-bye.

"Good night, Alex." "Good night, Eddie."

Eddie handed Alex her cake and she unlocked the door and walked into the house. The house was dark, so she assumed her mother had gone to bed. She tiptoed to the kitchen and put her cake in the refrigerator. Then she walked to her room and closed the door. As she was changing into her pajamas, she thought about the date. It was wonderful. Alex believed that she was beginning to fall for Eddie. She lay down in her bed and smiled. As she closed her eyes and drifted off to sleep, her head was filled with dreams of the wonderful and romantic Eddie James.

4

———

*A*lex put the last bag into the car and closed the trunk. She couldn't believe how quickly two weeks had flown by. By this time tomorrow, she would officially be a college student. For Alex, leaving home was bittersweet. She couldn't wait to experience college life, make new friends, and have new experiences, but she hated that she was leaving her mother alone. Her mom tried to put on a brave face for Alex, but she could tell that her leaving was breaking her mom's heart. She didn't want to leave her mom alone until she knew that she was going to be okay, but she also knew that it was time to leave the nest.

Her mom would be driving her to school in the morning to help her get settled before freshman orientation. Alex's uncle and grandfather would be following them to help unpack her belongings. She was looking forward to seeing Eddie again when she got to campus. He moved into an apartment about a week before freshmen were scheduled to move in. She missed him a lot and she was glad that the week was almost over.

Alex and Eddie went out several times after their first date and they always had a wonderful time. But Alex began to wonder about the status of their relationship. Whenever they went somewhere, they acted like a couple. They walked arm-in-arm, held hands, and were very affectionate toward each other, but they still didn't have a title. Alex was not in the habit of rushing things, but she couldn't deny that she had strong feelings for Eddie. She decided not to let the situation worry her and she would see how things went once they were together again.

Alex walked back into the house to grab a bottle of water. She began to look around her house and reminisce. She had lived in that house her entire life. Her height chart was still etched into the wall by the pantry door. Alex looked at the wall where she drew a picture of a princess and a castle when she was three. She remembered that her mom freaked out when she saw it. She made Alex stay in her room alone for what felt like hours to think about what she had done. Her father tried to paint over it, but even after two coats of paint, you could still see the large pink castle. Alex chuckled to herself; good times. Alex's mother walked in as she was taking a sip of water.

"You all ready to go, Miss Lady?" her mother asked, grabbing a bottle of water herself.

"Yea, everything's in the car."

"Good. What time is check-in?"

"10:00 a.m."

"Okay. What time do you want to leave?"

"Let's leave about six."

"I will make sure I'm up and ready by then," Michaela smiled.

"Good. Mom, I want to talk to you about something."

"What's that?"

"I'm worried about you, Mom."

"Oh Honey, don't worry about me. I'm fine."

"Are you really?"

"Yes."

"The reason I'm asking is because I'm leaving and you will be here by yourself."

"So?"

"What do you mean 'so'?" Alex asked with an obvious confused face. "Mom, you haven't been the same since Dad and Brian died."

"I know that, Honey."

"You do?"

"Yes, believe it or not, I'm not oblivious to my own emotions."

"So are you going to be okay?"

"Look, Alex, I know you're worried about me. I've been out of sorts for the last four years. I took your father and your brother's deaths really hard. But I've realized that I cannot sit around and be miserable forever. I will move on from this."

"What are you going to do?"

"Not sure yet. But seriously, don't worry about me. You have more important things to think about."

Alex gave her mom a hug. The conversation made her feel a lot better about leaving. She was glad that her mother was going to start working through her issues with her father's and brother's deaths. Alex tossed her bottle in the recycling bin and went into her room. She picked up the phone to call Eddie.

"Hey, Alex," he said when he picked up the phone.

"Hi, Eddie. How are you?"

"I'm good. Just picked up some dinner and about to settle in for the night."

"Yea, I ate before I packed up the car."

"So do you feel more comfortable with leaving?"

"Yea, my Mom and I had a nice little talk, so I feel a lot better."

"I'm glad. I can't wait to see you tomorrow."

"Really? I thought you would have been tired of me by now," Alex joked.

"I don't think I could ever get tired of you, Alex."

"Awwww, Eddie! That's so sweet."

"Yea, yea yea. Don't spread that around or people will think I'm whipped."

"Why do guys always worry about how other people view them?"

"When people think you have a weakness, they try to take advantage of it. That's why it's important to not show weakness."

"Everyone has weaknesses, Eddie."

"Yea, but only a fool advertises it."

"Right," Alex said, rolling her eyes. She thought it was best to leave that subject where it was because he was taking a kind remark way too seriously. "So are you coming over to help me unpack tomorrow morning?"

"What time are you getting here?"

"We should arrive around ten."

"And you're staying in Grant Hall, right?"

"Yea."

"All right, I'll see you in the morning. 10a.m. Grant Hall."

"Sounds good."

"Ok, miss you, Alex."

"Miss you too, Eddie. Bye."

Alex hung up the phone. She was glad that Eddie was com- ing to help her. He would get to meet her uncle and grandfather. She was especially interested in having Eddie meet her grandfather. He had an uncanny ability to read people and he was never wrong. She was hoping that he would validate all of the good feelings she had about Eddie.

Alex looked at the clock. It read 8:00 p.m. Alex wasn't tired but she decided to go to bed since she had a long day ahead of her. She kissed her mother goodnight and went to lie down in her bed. As she lay in the darkness, she slowly drifted to sleep thinking about all of the wonderful things she wanted to experience during her time in college.

5

"**G**ood morning, Precious," Alex's grandfather said, smiling as he walked into the kitchen, about a half an hour before they were supposed to leave for Pendleton University.

"Hey, Grandpa," Alex yawned.

"What's that yawn about? Didn't sleep well last night?" Alex's grandfather asked, before kissing her on the forehead.

Alex shook her head. She barely slept during the night. She kept tossing and turning. Alex wasn't sure if it was because she was anxious about leaving home or if she was just so excited about the new chapter in her life; either way, she was ready to get this day over with.

It was now 5:45 in the morning and everyone sat at the kitchen table waiting for Alex's uncle to arrive. She sat quietly and listened to the two adults talk about different things. Alex didn't get to see her grandfather that often. He lived about thirty minutes from Alex and her mom, but he was always traveling. He hung out with a group of people from his senior center and they took a lot of trips. Alex was happy to see him. She couldn't wait for them to catch up. He was telling her mom about his trip to Cancun when the three of them heard a horn blaring outside of the house.

"That must be George," Alex's mom sighed. George was her mom's younger brother. Their resemblance was so uncanny that the two often passed for identical twins. They both had the same oval face with brown eyes and thick curly hair. The only difference was in their build; George was tall and thin and Alex's mom was petite and plump.

Alex admired her uncle. He was a pastor at a church down the street from Alex's house. It seemed like if he wasn't at the church, he was at their house hanging out with her mom. George and Alex's mom got extremely close after the accident. He was an absolute godsend when they needed him and Alex was grateful for that. Alex, her grandfather, and her mother walked outside to greet George.

"You couldn't come to the door, George? Really? It's six in the morning! You'll wake the dead with that horn of yours." Alex's mother said to George as she gave him a hug.

"Good morning to you too, Mickey," George said calling Alex's mother, Michaela, by her nickname. "I didn't want us to be late getting on the road so I figured I would have everyone come out here. Plus, I come bearing gifts for the road." George pulled a cup holder out of his car. "Coffee for us and hot apple cider for my favorite niece since I know she doesn't drink coffee." George gave Alex a hug with his free arm. "You ready to go, Al?"

"Please, Uncle George, call me Alex. You know I hate that nickname."

"I know. That's why I love it." He winked at Alex and handed her the cider. "I brought bagels too. So everyone grab your drink and a bagel and let's hit the road. I don't want to put *Alex* behind schedule."

Everyone got into their respective cars and within five minutes, they were riding down the highway. Alex and her mother talked most of the way there. They reminisced about Alex's childhood and recalled a lot of memories about their family vacations. The time seemed to fly by and before Alex knew it, they were pulling into a parking space in front of her dormitory. She went into the building to check in and get her key. When she walked back outside to start unloading her things, Eddie was there talking to her mother. She wanted to run up to him and kiss him, but she didn't want to show her affection in front of her family. Her uncle and grandfather would never let her hear the end of it.

Alex quickly introduced everyone and they all grabbed bags and took the elevator up to Alex's room. After about thirty minutes, all of her belongings were in her room. She told Eddie she would see him when her family left and they parted ways. Her mother wanted to take her out to lunch before she left, so everyone piled into one car and they ate at a local restaurant. When lunch was over, they drove Alex back to her dormitory.

"Well...this is it," Alex said, staring up at the dormitory.

"Yes, it is," Alex's mother said, taking Alex's face in her hands. "My baby is leaving me." Tears began to stream down her face.

"Michaela, it's going to be okay. She isn't going to prison, just college," Alex's grandfather said, pulling her away from Alex.

"I know, Dad, but the day is really here. I'm going back home alone."

"Oh, Mickey," Alex's grandfather said, trying to console her. "It's going to be okay. You will see."

"I think it's time for us to go," George said, watching his sister in hysterics.

"I agree," Alex's grandfather said. "You take Michaela home and I will drive back alone." Alex's mother gave her a long hug that almost cut off her circulation and a kiss on the cheek. George hugged Alex and helped her mother into the car. Alex watched as they drove away. "Let's talk," Alex's grandfather said, putting his arm around Alex's neck.

"Okay."

"So this boy, Eddie?"

"Yea?"

"You met him back home?"

"Yea, I did. What do you think?"

"Alex, you know me. I read people."

"Yea, Grandpa. That's why I'm asking you what you think about him."

"I don't get good vibes from him, Alex."

"Really?"

"Yes. There's something about him. I can't put my finger on it and you know I am never wrong."

"I think you might be wrong this time, Grandpa. He's been a complete gentleman since I met him."

"I know you're going to do what you want to do, Alex, but I'm telling you, something is off. I don't trust him."

"Maybe you don't trust him because I'm your only grand-daughter, and you don't want to see me get hurt."

"You're right. I don't want my baby to get hurt. But do me a favor, keep an eye open. Okay?"

"Okay."

"Good girl." Alex's grandfather gave her a kiss and a hug. "I love you, baby. If you ever need anything, let me know."

"I will, Grandpa. Love you, too." Alex's grandfather got in his car and he was gone.

Alex thought about what her grandfather said to her while she walked to her room. Surely, he was wrong about Eddie. He was getting older now and he wasn't as sharp as he used to be. He probably just got those bad vibes because she's his only grand-child. If he could offer her some proof, she would be more inclined to believe him but all he had were vibes. Eddie had treated her wonderfully since the day they met. It just couldn't be possible that Eddie is bad news. Alex decided to shrug off her grandfather's warning. *In time, he will see that he's wrong about Eddie,* she thought.

Alex was about an hour into the unpacking process when Eddie came back to her room. He grabbed her by the waist and kissed her passionately. Oh, how Alex missed that! Now they were finally together. Alex couldn't wait to see where things would go. They let go of one another and Eddie helped Alex unpack her room.

"You have a lot of stuff," Eddie said, opening a medium- sized box marked 'School Supplies.' "Did you bring everything you own?"

"I'm supposed to bring everything I own. I live here now."

"Technically, you don't. You're just renting for about nine months."

"You know what I mean, Eddie. We're four hours from home. So if I want or need something, I can't just go back and get it."

"Yes, you could. I would drive you."

"It's an unnecessary trip. It's easier to just have everything here."

"I don't think it's all going to fit, babe." *Babe.* The word rang in Alex's ears. He hadn't called her "babe" before. Maybe that was a hint that they were a couple.

"Everything will fit, Eddie. Watch me work. I'm a master organizer."

"I'm sure you are, but on the off chance it doesn't all fit, you can keep some things at my place."

Alex stopped what she was doing and turned to look at Eddie. "Your place?"

"Yea, my place."

"No thanks, Eddie. I'm going to keep all my stuff here."

"Suit yourself, but I think we both know that you will be spending most of your time there anyway."

"What makes you say that?"

"Just a hunch."

"A hunch," Alex repeated after quickly glancing at Eddie. She went back to unpacking her things. "You talk like you can predict the future."

"No, I can't do that. But I do know enough to know that you and I will be spending a lot of time together."

"Time together as what?" Alex asked innocently. She was hoping that this was Eddie's way of confirming that they were a couple.

"As a couple."

Alex leaped for joy inside. This was the moment she had been waiting for. She nodded her head and tried to downplay her excitement. "So we are a couple now? Like, you're my boyfriend and I'm your girlfriend?"

"As long as you are willing."

"I'm willing," Alex shrugged. On the outside, Alex was trying desperately to play it cool in front of Eddie. But on the inside, she was doing cartwheels. She and Eddie were officially together.

"Good," Eddie said smiling. It was early evening when they finished unpacking all of Alex's things. Alex had to prepare for a floor meeting, so she and Eddie said good night to each other. She was having the perfect day. She and Eddie were officially a couple. She met her roommate and they seemed to get along well. Alex was really looking forward to her freshman year.

6

*I*t was a chilly night in November, and Alex was putting the finishing touches on her makeup. She and some friends from her dormitory were getting ready for a party. She couldn't wait to go. Adjustment to college life was more difficult than she thought it would be. She was so wrapped up in her studies that she rarely went out anywhere. She deserved this break.

"Oh, girl! I love that outfit! You're gonna be turnin' heads all night!" said Tameka as she walked into their room. Tameka Jamison was Alex's roommate and they became close instantly. She was a tall girl with an athletic build from Alabama. She had a short hair style, hazel eyes, and a thick country accent. Alex really valued their friendship. They both had the same major and were in a couple of the same classes together. Tameka definitely made the transition to college life more manageable for Alex.

"Thanks," Alex said before blotting her lips on a tissue.

"I'm glad you finally decided to come out with us. You never go anywhere."

"I know. I guess I'm not your typical freshman."

"I can see that. You study more than anyone I know."

"Well, we all can't be as brilliant as you, Tameka."

"You have a point," Tameka laughed. "But my brilliance isn't in my knowledge, it's in my time management skills."

"Yea, mine need to be better."

"I know. You spend every second of your free time with Eddie."

"So?"

"So…there are other aspects to college life than Eddie James."

"I know that."

"I know you know that, but I still felt like I should say it."

"Okay."

"So will Eddie be attendin' this party as well?"

"I'm not sure. He said he was going out tonight with some friends, but I'm not sure where they're going."

"So if he happens to be at the same party, will you be hangin' round him all night?"

"No. It's Girls' Night. I'm hanging with you."

"Good."

"Yea, I can always just see Eddie after the party."

"Oh, after the party? Gonna have a little late night romance, huh?"

"Sure, maybe some cuddling and talking."

"Cuddlin' and talkin'? Really?" Tameka asked in disbelief.

"Yea. We wouldn't do anything else."

"Wait a minute," Tameka said as if coming to an astounding epiphany. "You and Eddie haven't had sex yet?"

"No."

"Wow. I'm shocked."

"Why?"

"I mean, I just always assumed that you two had. You're always over there and it would've been rude of me to ask, so I assumed."

"I'm just not ready yet."

"Why not? You and Eddie have been hot and heavy since you got here."

"Because," Alex said, looking at the floor, "I'm a virgin."

"Okay?"

Alex looked up at Tameka. "That's all you have to say?"

"What else am I supposed to say? It's not a bad thing to be a virgin, Alex."

"I don't know. Whenever I tell people I'm a virgin, they either think it's sad or they laugh at me."

"Really? Well, that's rude."

"Tell me about it."

"Does Eddie know?"

"Yes, and he's been really patient with me."

"Then I see no problem. You'll do it when you feel like you're ready."

"I know."

"Okay, so enough with the sex talk. Let's get outta here. Ladies free till eleven."

Alex grabbed her clutch, and she and Tameka left for the party. They arrived at the party and the place was packed. Alex, Tameka, and the rest of the girls had to push their way through the crowd to find a table to sit at.

"This party is hype!" one of the girls said, waving her hands in the air.

"Yea, it is," Tameka said. "What do you think, Alex?"

"I think we should go dance!" Alex said, standing up from the table and grabbing a guy from the wall. Alex danced nonstop for several songs. She was having a great time.

Around midnight, Alex saw Eddie walk into the party. He was

with several of his friends, so she decided to keep her distance and continue dancing. About half an hour from the time she saw Eddie enter the party, Tameka tapped Alex on her shoulder.

"Do you know that Eddie is staring at you?" she asked with an odd look on her face.

"What?" Alex said, looking around. "No, I didn't know that. Where is he?"

"Over there. And he looks pissed." Tameka pointed to a wall where Eddie stood with his friends. Through the darkness, he seemed to be glaring at her.

"Wow, he does look pissed. I wonder what's wrong. I'm going to go see what's wrong with him."

"Okay, but remember, it's Girls' Night."

"I know. I'll be back." Tameka kept on dancing beside the other girls and Alex made her way over to the wall. When she got close to Eddie, he seemed to be shooting daggers at her with his eyes. "Hi, baby," she said, putting her arms around his neck and attempting to kiss him. Eddie turned his cheek toward her and pulled her arms from around his neck. Alex was becoming concerned. "What's wrong, Eddie?"

"How could you?" he asked. Alex could smell alcohol on his breath.

"What are you talking about, Eddie?"

"How could you embarrass me like this?"

"Embarrass you? What did I do?"

"You are in this club wearing that slutty outfit and dancing with all these guys. What are you some kind of whore?"

Alex's eyeballs bulged. She couldn't believe that Eddie was talking to her like that. "You're drunk, Eddie. You don't know what you're saying."

"Oh, I know exactly what I'm saying, Alex. How could you disrespect me like this?"

"Look, Eddie.This is the wrong place to have this conversation. Let's talk about it more when you're sober."

Alex turned to leave, but Eddie grabbed her arm. "Where do you think you're going?"

"Back to my friends," Alex said, snatching her arm from Eddie's grip.

"No, you're not. You're going to stay here with me until this party ends."

"No, I'm not."

"Fine. Then I'm taking you back to your room so you can change."

"I'm not going anywhere with you, Eddie. I'm going back over to my friends now. Good night."

Alex fought tears as she walked back over to her friends. How could Eddie speak to her that way? He was always so good to her. She wasn't sure if it was the alcohol or Eddie showing his true colors. When Alex got back to the table, Tameka sensed something was wrong and asked if she was alright. Alex nodded and told her that she would tell her the whole story later. After Alex calmed down, she got up and danced until the party was over.

On the way home, she began to feel anxious about the conversation she was going to have with Eddie the next day. He couldn't possibly have meant those horrible things that he said to her. Part of Alex hoped it was the alcohol making Eddie say all of those cruel things. Alex wouldn't know for sure until she talked to him about it. She decided to put the incident out of her mind and go to sleep. Tomorrow would take care of itself.

lex woke up early the next morning to take a jog. She had to clear her mind before she talked to Eddie. All night long, Alex tossed and turned thinking about how she would start the conversation. She didn't want to hurt Eddie's feelings, but she also didn't want to be spoken to so harshly. She debated ideas in her head while she jogged a mile from campus. By the time she got back to her room, her mind was at ease. She knew how she wanted to approach the conversation and she made up in her mind that whatever the results were, she would accept them. Alex showered and threw on an outfit. She planned to grab some breakfast and head over to Eddie's. She was sure that he was probably still asleep, but she had to get the conversation over with.

Alex arrived at Eddie's apartment around ten in the morning. She was surprised when he answered the door in high spirits. He actually looked refreshed like he had a good night's rest and he wasn't showing any signs of a hangover. Alex walked into the apartment and sat on the couch.

"Hey, babe. I made some eggs and bacon. You want some?" Eddie asked, walking into his kitchen.

"No, I'm good."

"Okay." Eddie hummed while he fixed himself a plate.

Alex still couldn't get over his good mood. "I'm surprised you aren't hung over from last night," she said slowly.

"Don't be. I know how to hold my liquor."

"Right," Alex said, rolling her eyes.

"So I'm assuming you're here to talk about last night?"

"So you remember?"

"I forget very little, Alex," Eddie said, sitting down at the table. "Come join me, please." Alex went and sat down at the table with Eddie. "What's on your mind?" he asked.

"Do you remember how you talked to me last night?"

"Remind me."

"I thought you said you forget very little," Alex said, sarcastically.

"Okay, let me rephrase. Tell me what I said that bothered you."

"Oh, I don't know, Eddie," Alex said, slightly annoyed. "How about telling me I was embarrassing you? Or, worse, telling me I looked slutty and asking me if I was some kind of whore?"

"Ah," Eddie said, knowingly.

"So you have nothing else to say but 'ah'?"

"Tell me what I was supposed to think, Alex. You were out there wearing something that, in my personal opinion, looked like something that you should wear for me behind closed doors. Then on top of that, I see you dancing in that suggestive outfit with all these guys. People know you're my girl. So when you go somewhere, you represent me. I just believe that you could have worn something a little more tasteful and carried yourself with a little more class."

Alex's eyes widened. She expected Eddie to be apologetic,

begging her for forgiveness. Instead, he was defending himself. She couldn't believe what she was hearing. Alex sat in silence for a few minutes, taking in what Eddie just said to her. "So you aren't going to apologize?" she finally asked.

"For hurting your feelings, yes. For saying what I said, no," he said, quietly. Alex felt like she was going to cry. This couldn't really be coming out of Eddie's mouth. Alex got up from the table and went to sit on the couch. Eddie finished his breakfast and joined her. She turned her face from him.

"Look at me, babe," Eddie said, softly. Alex turned her head to look at him. "I really am sorry that I hurt your feelings. I let my emotions get the best of me, and I should have found a better way to convey what I was feeling. I don't want to lose you over something like this. I love you."

Alex turned her entire body toward Eddie. "I love you, too." They kissed.

"Just do me a favor," he said, slowly.

"What's that?" Alex asked.

"Don't wear anything like that again unless you go somewhere with me."

"Why not?"

"Because I want to be the only one around you when you have on something that body-hugging."

Alex fought a smile. She was still a little upset with Eddie. "I'm going to wear what I want to wear, when I want to wear it."

"Okay then, let's compromise. If you wear something like that again, run it by me first, as a warning. That way, I won't be as upset."

"Okay, I can do that," Alex smiled.

"Also, I only want you to dance with me from now on," Eddie said, staring into Alex's eyes.

"So you're telling me that I can't dance with anyone else?"

"If we're at the same party, no."

"Come on, Eddie, that's ridiculous. I don't care who you dance with. It's just dancing."

"But I do care."

"I still don't see why it matters."

"It matters because it would make me feel better," he urged. "Look, it's simple. If we're at the same party, we dance with each other. If we're there alone, we dance with whomever we want to dance with. Sound good?"

"Fine," Alex agreed, reluctantly.

"Good, glad we could come to an agreement." The two kissed again. "You know," Eddie said seductively, "this would be the perfect time for make-up sex."

"I'm sure it would if we were having sex."

"You can't blame a guy for trying. Let's watch a movie and then we can go grab some lunch."

"Okay," Alex said. She barely paid attention as the movie played. She wasn't sure what to make of their conversation. She was happy that she and Eddie had professed their love for one another, but she didn't like the fact that Eddie felt like he had a right to say the awful things he said.

Suddenly, Alex remembered the warning her grandfather gave on her first day at Pendleton. Surely this couldn't have been what her grandfather was talking about when he warned her about Eddie. Alex didn't know what to think. She decided to shrug off her feelings of angst and pay attention to the movie. Surely, Eddie wouldn't act like that again; especially since they came to a compromise. Alex laid her head on Eddie's shoulder and enjoyed the rest of the movie.

8

A few weeks had gone by since the incident at the party and everything seemed like it was back to normal. Eddie was being the wonderful man that Alex knew he could be, and they were becoming even closer. They began to discuss taking their relationship to the next level, and Alex felt like she was finally ready to take that step. So she and Eddie planned the entire event.

It would happen over Christmas break. After exams, Alex would stay with Eddie for a few days and they would make love. Eddie was excited that Alex was ready. He said that he wanted her to be comfortable in the situation but waiting was beginning to wear on him. The day before she was supposed to go over to Eddie's apartment, she began to get nervous. *What was it going to be like? Was it going to hurt? Would Eddie be patient with her then too?* Alex had so many questions in her mind that could only be answered by the actual event itself.

After her last exam, Alex checked out of her room for the holiday break and went over to Eddie's apartment. Her mind was racing. She hoped she wouldn't get so nervous that she would chicken out.

When Eddie answered the door, she was invited in. They talked for a while and watched some movies. Then Eddie took her out to dinner. Alex was becoming more and more anxious. She was starting to feel like she just wanted to get the whole thing over with. Finally, the time came.

Eddie and Alex went back to his apartment after dinner. He said that he was going to take a shower and he asked her to join him. *So this is it,* Alex thought as she made her way to the bathroom. *I won't be a virgin after tonight.* She slowly undressed as Eddie turned on the water and stepped into the shower. *What was shower sex going to be like?* She had hoped that she would lose her virginity in a bed. As Alex showered, she was somewhat surprised at Eddie. He wasn't trying anything. All he did was wash. *Okay, this must not be it then,* Alex thought.

When they were done in the shower, they dried off, and Eddie gave Alex a box. He asked her to wear what was in the box and when she was ready, to meet him in the bedroom. After he walked out and closed the door, Alex looked in the box. It was a lacy, powder blue underwear set.

Alex sat on the edge of the bathtub and stared at it. She was already naked and she didn't understand the point of putting on something that was going to be on the floor in a few minutes. She put on the underwear set anyway and began to pace back and forth in the bathroom. She felt like she was about to chicken out. "Okay, Alex, you're a big girl," she whispered to herself. "You love Eddie and you're ready for this." Alex took a deep breath and exited the bathroom.

When she walked into Eddie's bedroom, he was sitting on the edge of the bed waiting for her. He smiled and walked over to her. As he slowly began to kiss her neck, Alex looked around. There were candles burning around the room and there was soft music coming from the stereo. She would have enjoyed the romantic scene more if she hadn't let her nerves get the best of her. She pushed Eddie away and sat down on the bed.

"What's wrong?" he asked, sitting down beside her.

"I don't know if I can do this, Eddie. I'm so nervous."

"Don't be nervous, Babe. I've got you. I'm not going to hurt you."

"So it doesn't hurt?"

"Well, to be honest, Alex, there could be some discomfort when we first start."

"Discomfort?" Alex repeated, nervously.

"Yes, discomfort. But after a few seconds, you should be fine." Alex let out a nervous sigh. "Look, babe," Eddie said, reassuringly, "we will take it as slow as you want to take it. And if at any point, you become uncomfortable and want to stop, just say the word."

Alex smiled. "Okay."

Eddie took her hand in his and kissed Alex on her cheek. She was glad that she and Eddie talked; it made her feel a lot better. He escorted her to the head of the bed where they laid side by side and began to kiss. Eddie was being so gentle with her, and it made Alex feel amazing. Before she knew it, Alex felt her virginity slipping away. She couldn't believe that this moment was finally here. She wanted to laugh at herself for being so nervous about something that was clearly so wonderful.

When it was over, Alex lay in Eddie's arms staring at the ceiling. The fact that she was no longer a virgin kept replaying in her mind. Alex always wondered how she would feel after it finally happened. She wondered if she would regret it or feel different. But she didn't regret losing her virginity to Eddie. She was content and she was in love. There could be no better feeling than that.

∼

OVER THE NEXT FEW DAYS, Alex and Eddie made love on and off. Alex was really enjoying herself, and she hoped Eddie was too. But soon something happened to Alex that terrified her. It was the night before she and Eddie were going to ride home together. They were making love as they had the past few days and at first, everything was fine. Then Eddie did something to Alex that made her extremely uncomfortable. Alex asked Eddie to stop. He ignored her. So Alex spoke a little louder because she wasn't sure if he could hear her.

"Eddie, stop. That hurts," Alex said. Eddie still ignored her. She tried to push him off her, but Eddie grabbed her wrists and pinned them to the bed. Alex couldn't move and she was getting scared. "Eddie, stop!" she said again while trying to pull her wrists free. Eddie lowered his torso down on top of Alex's chest and said, "Stop, moving."

Alex was mortified. She couldn't believe that he was actually hurting her. Just a few days before, he promised to stop if something became uncomfortable. Now, he wouldn't stop, even though she was in pain. Alex winced from her discomfort and she tried to hold back her tears. She couldn't believe that this was happening to her.

Alex lay there for what felt like hours. Finally, Eddie rolled off her, got up, and went to the bathroom. He didn't say a word to her. She looked over at the clock and saw that it had only been five minutes since she asked Eddie to stop. Alex couldn't believe Eddie would do this to her. She rolled over into the fetal position as the tears slid down her face. She trusted him with her body and he betrayed her trust.

Eddie walked back into the room and got into the bed. He

pulled Alex close to him and kissed her on the back of her neck. "I love you," he said, rubbing her back.

Alex quickly wiped the tears from her face and rolled to face him. "I love you too," she said, forcing a smile. Eddie put his arms around her to hold her, but Alex moved away.

"I'm going to take a shower before I go to sleep," she said, getting up rather quickly from the bed.

"Okay, I'll join you," Eddie said sitting up.

"No, it's okay. Stay there. I'll be back in a few minutes."

"All right, don't stay in there too long. I don't want to get lonely," Eddie smiled.

Alex nodded and went into the bathroom. After she locked the door, Alex turned on the shower and let the water run. She sat on the toilet lid for a few minutes, trying to make sense of what happened. She didn't like not being able to move or Eddie refusing to stop when she asked him to. It was the first time in her life that she felt truly helpless.

She kept trying to rationalize the situation in her head. Maybe he just didn't hear her. Or maybe he thought Alex was teasing him and really wanted him to keep going. No matter what excuse Alex tried to make for the situation, it didn't help. When she said stop, he should have stopped.

Alex got into the bathtub and sat under the spraying water. She couldn't be in a relationship like this; and she wasn't going to be if Eddie tried that again. Alex decided that she would talk to Eddie about it on the way home. She turned off the shower and went back into the bedroom. After she closed the door, she was relieved to see that Eddie was asleep. She crept over to the bed and got in. With her back to Eddie, she drifted into a fitful sleep.

9

***

They were about two hours from their hometown when Alex brought up the incident that happened the night before. She approached the subject gingerly because she wasn't sure how Eddie was going to react.

"So…what did you think about last night?" Alex asked, slowly.

"It was wonderful like always," Eddie smiled. "What did you think?"

"It started out good but—"

"But?" Eddie interrupted.

"Yea. It didn't end that way, though."

Eddie glanced over at Alex then turned his eyes back to the road. "I liked the ending," he said.

"You did?"

"Yea."

"Eddie, you were hurting me."

"Hurting you," Eddie repeated as more of a statement than a question. Alex noticed that he had a really nonchalant attitude. It almost seemed as if he didn't care.

"Yes. You were hurting me."

"Hurting you?" he repeated again with his same attitude.

"Yes," Alex said, puzzled by Eddie's behavior. She had never seen this side of him before. He was strangely calm. "I asked you to stop and you wouldn't. Then when I tried to push you away, you pinned me down." Alex waited for Eddie to say something, but he drove in silence. "I didn't like that at all," Alex continued," and I won't deal with it again."

Eddie nodded, but still remained silent. Alex was becoming upset. She felt like Eddie wasn't listening to her. "You have nothing to say?" she asked.

"Waiting for you to finish," he said, quietly.

"I'm done."

"So, you want to break up? Is that what this conversation is about?"

"No. I'm trying to tell you I didn't like what happened last night."

"So now you don't enjoy the way I make love to you?"

"Eddie, you're twisting my words."

"Look, Alex. I love it when we're together. I love making love to you and I love you. I don't want you to be unsatisfied."

"I'm not unsatisfied, Eddie. I just want you to listen to me when I say stop and I don't want you to hold me down anymore."

"I apologize for that, Babe. I must have gotten caught up in the moment. Being with you is just so incredible."

"Thanks, Eddie. I enjoy being with you too, just not like that."

"Noted."

"So you won't do it again?"

"I'll try not to."

"You'll try not to?" Alex retorted.

"Yes, try not to," Eddie repeated.

"What is that supposed to mean, Eddie?"

"It means what I said, Alex. It's hard to control what I do when I'm making love to you. It's so easy to get lost in the moment. So like I said, I'll try."

"Eddie, if it happens again, I won't be able to continue in this relationship," Alex asserted. Eddie gave Alex a look that sent chills down her spine. When he turned to look at the road again, he said, "Alex, you're not going to leave me."

"Seriously, Eddie. If what happened last night happens again, I will."

"No *I'm* serious, Alex," Eddie said, his voice tense. "You aren't going anywhere."

"You have no control over what I will and will not do."

"Oh, Alex," Eddie chuckled," I may not have control over your actions, but I do have control over something."

"Oh really?"

"Yea."

"And what is that?"

"Your heart. See, your heart is mine now and because of that, I know that you won't leave me."

"Don't be so sure about that, Eddie."

"I am sure, Alex, and you are too. What we have is forever. You're mine and I'm yours. Now, I said I would try; you have my word on that. So relax for the rest of the trip, all right?"

Alex turned to face the window. There was nothing else to be said. She told Eddie how she felt and the conversation turned in a completely different direction. Alex shuddered and crossed her arms, in an effort to ward off the chill in the car. The things Eddie said during their disagreements were beginning to bother her. She hoped his statement about her not leaving him was based on the fact that he knew Alex had deep feelings for him; however, it seemed as if he was dictating an order rather than stating an observation. Alex wasn't sure what to think. All she knew was that she did love Eddie and she wanted the relationship to work. He did say he would try to refrain from doing what he did to her the night before. Alex had faith that Eddie was telling the truth and she chose to believe that. After all, there was no way Eddie would go back on his word when he knew their relationship was on the line.

*O*ver the Christmas break, Alex was glad to be on positive terms with Eddie. They saw each other frequently and Alex was glad that Eddie was back to himself. Lately, he seemed as if he was on edge with the party and sex incidents, but Alex just associated that with the stress of school. While he was at home, he seemed happy and carefree. He was an incredibly loving and doting boyfriend. Alex rode back to school with Eddie with high hopes for their relationship. She buried his past transgressions in her mind and looked forward to building their future together.

About a week after classes started, Eddie began to act out of his usual charming character. He seemed stressed and he was extremely touchy. Alex felt like she had to walk on eggshells when she was around him. She wasn't sure what was going on with Eddie, but Alex decided that she was going to keep her distance until this phase blew over. Alex went to her classes and hung out with her friends. She was glad to have a little extra freedom. She was beginning to see how much of her time she actually gave to

Eddie. So she vowed to manage her time better so that she could include all the activities into her schedule.

One afternoon in early February, Alex exited the sociology building after her 1:00 p.m. class ended. She was headed back to her dorm room to study when she spotted a guy from her calculus class. She stopped to speak.

"Hi, Darrell, how are you?" Alex asked with a smile. Darrell Hopkins was a math wizard. It seemed like he could ace all of the assignments without even studying.

"Hey, Alex. I'm good. 'Bout to go study for our first calc test."

"Wow, you actually study? I thought you could do all of the equations in your head."

"I usually can, but better safe than sorry, right?"

"Yea, that's true. I need to study, too. Unfortunately, I'm not as brilliant as you are."

"Nonsense. You're more brilliant than you realize." Darrell smiled at her. She had always assumed that he had a crush on her from the moment she walked into the calculus class. He was always so nice to her and he was always offering to help her with the work.

Darrell was a very attractive guy. He was six feet, six inches tall with green eyes and he played basketball for the university. Alex would have actually attempted to date him if she wasn't committed to Eddie. But even though she had a boyfriend, there was nothing wrong with a little harmless flirting.

"Thank you," she said, giving Darrell a shy smile.

"So where are you headed?" Darrell asked.

"Back to my room."

"Oh, okay. I could walk you there, if you like."

"I don't know, Darrell. I don't want you going out of your way."

"Where are you staying?"

"I'm in Grant Hall."

"You're not out of my way. I'm across from you in Artmore."

"Well, okay then, you can walk me," Alex smiled.

Alex and Darrell began to walk toward their dormitories. They laughed and got to know one another better. Alex discovered that they actually had a lot in common. When they got to the walkway that separated their dorms, they said good-bye and parted ways. *Darrell is a really nice guy,* Alex thought. *Maybe I will try to hook him up with Tameka.* When Alex got to her room, she immediately began studying.

About an hour after she started studying, her phone rang. She looked at the caller id. It was Eddie. She wanted to ignore the call and continue studying, but she had been avoiding him recently so she decided it was time to talk.

"Hey, Eddie," Alex said, picking up the phone.

"Hey," Eddie said. "I need you to come over here." He sounded angry.

"Why, thank you for asking about my day," Alex retorted. "It was good. How was yours?" She was really getting tired of Eddie's attitude.

"I'm serious, Alex. You need to come over here."

"I'm studying, Eddie."

"Now, Alex!" Eddie yelled, before hanging up the phone.

Alex was shocked and a little scared. She had no idea what could have made him angry enough to yell at her over the phone. Alex let out a heavy sigh. She decided that she had better get over to his apartment before he became angrier and decided to come find her. Because if he did come looking for her, she wouldn't get any studying done. Alex put her books in her bag and left to see Eddie. As she walked, she became more and more frustrated. Eddie seemed to have some severe emotional issues. He was yelling at her for reasons that only he knew about, and he just seemed so hostile for reasons beyond her comprehension. This man she was dating now was nothing like the man she fell in love with. Maybe it was time for the relationship to come to an end.

When Alex got to Eddie's front door, he opened it before she had a chance to knock. She walked in and sat on the couch. Eddie stood in front of her. He looked like his blood was boiling. "Is there something you need to tell me, Alex?" he asked as if trying to remain calm.

"Yes. You are interfering with my study time," Alex said, clearly irritated.

"I'm not playing, Alex."

"Neither am I. I have an exam coming up."

"Last chance. Is there anything that you need to tell me?"

"No, Eddie."

"You're such a liar."

"Excuse me?"

"You heard me."

"All right, I don't know what you're mad at today, but I didn't do anything wrong. So I'm going to go." Alex picked up her bag to leave.

"You're not going anywhere," Eddie said, grabbing the bag and throwing it across the room. Alex sat on the couch, staring at Eddie. She was horrified. Something had to be terribly wrong.

"Look, Eddie," Alex said slowly, "I'm not sure what I did to upset you—"

"Oh, you know exactly what you did," Eddie interrupted.

"I'm honestly clueless, Eddie. Can you please tell me what's going on?"

"Did you really think I wouldn't find out about your little boyfriend?"

"Boyfriend?" Alex asked clearly puzzled. "Eddie, what are you talking about? *You* are my boyfriend."

"I'm talking about Darren Hodgkins, the basketball player."

"You mean, *Darrell Hopkins?*" Alex asked.

"So you admit it. You've been cheating on me."

"Eddie, I'm not cheating on you. Darrell is just a guy from my Calc class."

"Don't lie to me, Alex. I know you've been doing something behind my back. It all adds up. You've been avoiding. You act like you don't want to be around me. Then today, one of my friends sees you with this basketball freak of nature. You don't want to be with me. You don't love me. You're trying to move on to the next guy and you weren't even woman enough to come and tell me. I had to hear it from somebody else. You're shameful, Alex…just shameful. You make me sick. I hope you and your new boyfriend will be happy together 'cause I'm moving on too. Do you know how many women would love to be with Edward Steven James, huh? Do you recognize how lucky you are that I even wanted to be with you? I can have any woman I want, but I chose you. You would think after all I have done for you that you could show a little gratitude. But no, you can't do that. You're heartless, Alex. Go be with your boy, but I will tell you this, he will never love you like I do." Eddie paused. "So you don't have anything to say? Won't speak up for yourself now that you got caught?"

Alex was mortified. She could not believe that Eddie was acting in such a manner, especially over something that wasn't true. Alex kept trying to figure out what was going through Eddie's mind that would lead him to such outlandish conclusions, but she had no luck. All she could think to say was, "Eddie, I'm not cheating on you." Tears began streaming down her face.

"Then why were you with this guy, Alex?"

"I saw him on the way back to my dorm. He lives in Artmore, so we walked together."

"And that's all it was?"

"Yes. That's all."

"Then why have you been avoiding me lately? You act like you don't have time for me anymore."

"Because you've been agitated and having rants like the one you just had. I feel like I've been walking on eggshells with you."

"I'm sorry, babe. I've just got a lot on my plate right now. Then you start making yourself scarce and I hear about you with some dude, I just lost it. I don't want to lose you, Alex. I can't imagine life without you. I love you."

"I love you too, Eddie, but love can only take a relationship so far. We have to be able to communicate with each other without you going off on me for no reason. You really hurt my feelings."

"I know, Alex, and I'm sorry. I really am. Let me make it up to you."

"How?"

"Dinner. And maybe later, some making up."

"Making up? Does everything have to end with sex?"

"No, but it's been a while and you can't blame me for asking."

"Rain check on the dinner. I really have to study. Just do me a favor?"

"What's that?"

"Promise me you won't act like that anymore."

"You have my word."

"Okay."

"So you forgive me?"

"Yes, I forgive you."

"Good."

Eddie went over to give Alex a hug and a kiss. She was glad

that they were able to get the situation straightened out. She wiped the tears from her face and got up from the couch. When she left Eddie's apartment to finish studying, she had high hopes that things would get better. She was sure once Eddie was past whatever was stressing him, he would be back to normal.

11

*A*lex was relieved when April came around. The weather became warmer and trees were beginning to bloom. The semester had been very difficult for Alex to handle. She was carrying a full load, which meant that she practically lived in the library, and she had to deal with Eddie's emotional peaks and valleys. Sometimes, he was so wonderful to her; it reminded Alex of his sweet and wonderful demeanor in the beginning. Other times, he was cold, distant, and could be vicious at times. He would call Alex horrible names and criticize everything that she did. But he would always apologize and return to his charming self for a little while.

It was the good times that kept Alex going. She kept hoping that the good moments were the end of Eddie's tirades, but Alex would be disappointed every time. Alex was getting tired of riding this emotional rollercoaster with Eddie and she knew that if the relationship continued in the same manner, she would have to get off.

Alex was preparing to go to the library one evening to study for her sociology final, when she realized that she couldn't find the book she needed. She looked in all of her desk drawers and under her bed, but it wasn't in either place. Then it dawned on her; she left it at Eddie's. She finished putting her things into her bag and sprinted over to Eddie's apartment. She wanted to get in and out so she could start studying. She knocked on the door and waited. Nothing. So she knocked again. Still nothing. *That's weird,* Alex thought to herself.

She scanned the parking lot and saw that Eddie's car was there. If his car was there, why wouldn't he answer the door? Alex tried the knob and found that the door was unlocked. She let herself in. All she had to do was grab her book off Eddie's kitchen table. When she was putting the book in her bag, she saw Eddie walk out of his bedroom.

"Hi, babe," Alex said, going over to give Eddie a quick hug. "I just stopped by to grab my book. I hope you don't mind, I let myself in."

Eddie looked shocked to see her. "I didn't know I left the door unlocked," he said, looking behind him. "I thought you were going to be in the library."

"Yea, I'm on my way there now. I just really needed this book."

"Okay. Well, you got it. See you later."

Alex got the feeling that Eddie was trying to rush her out of his apartment. Usually, when she prepared to leave, he would always come up with some reason why he wanted her to stay. Something wasn't right.

"What's going on, Eddie? Why are you trying to rush me out of your apartment?" Alex asked. Eddie didn't say a word. Alex was no fool. She knew something was up. She began to look around the room for clues. Then it dawned on her. Eddie was shirtless when he came out of his room and he closed the door behind him; he never did that. There had to be someone in his bedroom.

Alex walked past Eddie and opened the door. She saw a girl in the room putting her clothes on. The girl paused when she saw Alex and then sped up the dressing process. Alex felt sick to her stomach. She turned around and looked at Eddie. He was leaning on the wall drinking a cup of juice. Alex couldn't figure out how he could possibly be so calm when she just caught him cheating on her.

"So this is how it is, Eddie? You're cheating on me?"

Eddie sipped his juice and said, "Symone, go home."

Alex watched the girl as she quickly walked to the door. "You don't have to tell me twice," she said, under her breath. When the door was closed, Alex sat down on the couch. She was beginning to feel lightheaded.

"How could you do this to me?" Alex asked, trying to fight tears. "I've been faithful to you and I have loved you. I gave you my virginity and this is how you treat me? Am I just one of many now?"

"No, there's you and then there's her," he said.

"So what now? You want to have two girlfriends?"

"Symone isn't my girlfriend. She's just a jump off."

"A jump off?"

"Yea. I tell her to jump on it and she gets me off."

"That's disgusting."

"Well, it's her job. That's what hoes do."

"So you've been having sex with this girl at the same time you've been having sex with me?"

"What sex, Alex? It's like I have to beg you to give me some. It seems like you can make time for everything else, but you can't make time for me."

"So now it's my fault that you're having sex with someone else?"

"Might as well be," Eddie huffed.

"Fine, since Symone is giving you what you want, why don't you just go and be with her?"

Eddie laughed. "I'm not trying to be with that girl. She's a trampoline for half the men on campus. As soon as I get off, another man will hop on."

Alex gagged. "Oh my goodness, now I have to get myself checked for STIs."

"No, you're good. Everything I did with her was protected."

"I can't believe you cheated on me with some jump off. And on top of that, you're sitting here talking to me about it like I'm one of your friends."

"If you were one of my friends," Eddie said, "this would be a completely different conversation."

"I can only imagine," Alex said, rolling her eyes.

"Look, I really don't know what I'm supposed to say, Alex. I honestly didn't expect to get caught."

"You didn't expect to get caught? Do you hear yourself right now?"

"It's like I said before. You weren't doing your job, so I found someone to do it for you. You should be grateful."

Alex's jaw dropped. "I should be grateful that I got cheated on? Really?"

"Look, this conversation is going nowhere. Why don't we just get down to the heart of the matter? Are you going to give me more sex or not?"

"As far as I'm concerned, you will never touch me again."

"If we're going to be together, we're going to have sex. That just isn't negotiable in this relationship."

"Then I guess there is no relationship, Eddie."

Eddie stared at Alex for a moment. Then he said, "Clearly, you need a few days to think this over."

"It's nothing to think about, Eddie. I'm done."

"Eddie laughed. "Alex, I've told you before, you aren't going to leave me. Did you think I was joking when I said that? Because if you did, you're really stupid."

"Excuse me?"

"I didn't stutter. Look, Alex, I love you and we're going to be together for the long term."

"Are you really telling me I can't break up with you?"

"I'm telling you that you're not going to. Let's face it, Alex, we both know you won't leave me. You love me too much to leave me and I know you want us to work. And in the back of your mind, you know that if you leave me, you will never find anyone else like me. You won't find anyone to love you like I do or hold you down financially like I do. So do us both a favor and stop threatening to leave me."

So many things were going through Alex's head. She really did love Eddie, but she wasn't willing to be in a relationship like this. He was rude to her and he was blatantly cheating on her. Alex couldn't bare to think about what Eddie might do next. She also didn't know if she could trust him anymore, or if she should even try.

"I do want to be with you, Eddie. But I can't be with you when there are other females involved."

"I'm nineteen years old, Alex. I want sex. If I'm not getting it from you, then it has to come from somewhere. So please, just do your job and make sure I'm taken care of."

"How am I supposed to do that, Eddie? Our schedules are crazy right now as it is."

"So move in with me."

"Are you serious?"

"Yea."

"I'm not doing that, Eddie. We've barely been together a year. It's too soon."

"Suit yourself, Alex. It's a good option with our crazy schedules. But hey, if you're uncomfortable, live in the dorm."

"Will you cheat on me again?"

"Up to you."

"I really can't move in with you, Eddie," Alex whined.

"Like I said, it's up to you. I'm not going to beg you. You're a smart girl though, so you need to figure something out."

Alex looked at her watch and realized how late it was. "I really have to go study, Eddie."

"Yea, you go do that. I can't have you flunking out of school," he chuckled. Alex picked up her bag and headed toward the door. "Oh, Alex?" Eddie called after her.

"Yes, Eddie."

"I want you to come back when you're finished."

"Why?"

"You know why."

Alex sighed. "Really? Symone didn't finish the job?"

"I want it from you."

"I can't, Eddie. I just caught you cheating. I'm not ready to give myself to you again."

"You have your entire study session to get ready or I make a phone call."

Alex nodded and walked out of the apartment. There was just no way she was going to be ready by the time she was finished studying. The thought of Eddie being with that other girl turned Alex's stomach. She couldn't believe that he would cheat on her. She had trusted him wholeheartedly with everything that was in her and he betrayed that trust.

Alex wanted to take a shower. The entire conversation made her feel dirty. She cringed every time she thought about going back to Eddie's apartment. If she didn't, she knew that Symone girl would be right back over there doing god-knows-what to him. Alex decided that if she really wanted to be with Eddie, she was going to have to figure out a way to keep him satisfied. And even though the thought of making love to Eddie repulsed her at the moment, she knew that she was going to have to go back over there when she was finished studying. She didn't feel like there was much of a choice at this point. She wouldn't leave Eddie because she loved him and if she didn't do her "job," he was going to get someone else to do it. She didn't want to move in with Eddie, but it seemed that was her only option. When Alex came to that conclusion, she cried.

12

---

*A*lex sat in the library and watched the clock. It was almost four in the morning and Alex was exhausted. She didn't need to study that long for her exam, but she intentionally pulled an all-nighter to avoid going back to Eddie's apartment. She hoped that he would be asleep by the time she got there and that he didn't make a certain phone call.

The whole situation bothered her. It almost seemed like Eddie was bragging about cheating on her. Alex was truly disgusted. She had put everything she had into her relationship with Eddie. Whatever free time she had after studying and extracurricular activities went to him. She really didn't understand why he was doing this to her and giving her ultimatums. It just didn't seem right.

Alex told herself that she was going to leave at exactly 4:00 a.m. She watched the clock as the second hand counted down to the dreaded hour. Five...four...three...two...one...time to go. She packed her things and walked out of the library. When she arrived at Eddie's apartment, it took him a while to answer the door. Alex's stomach was in knots. She was hoping that she didn't come around during another Eddie/Symone interaction. After about two minutes, Eddie answered the door. He looked like he had been sleeping. *Good,* Alex thought. *Maybe I won't have to do anything tonight after all.* She walked in and put her things by the couch. When she walked into the bedroom, Eddie was fast asleep. Alex let out a sigh of relief. She was so glad that she didn't have to have sex with Eddie. She got into the bed and laid there staring at the ceiling.

Her skin crawled with every thought of Eddie having a girl in the bed she was lying in. She wondered if he even changed his sheets before she got there. Alex knew there was no way she was going to be able to sleep if she stayed in the bed with Eddie so she went and laid on the couch. *Finally, I can get some sleep,* Alex thought as she drifted off to sleep.

When Alex woke up a few hours later, she told Eddie about her decision to move in with him. His reaction puzzled her. He didn't express any feelings of happiness toward the news; his demeanor was more like that of a spoiled child who finally got their way. Since the semester was almost over and they were both going home for the summer, Alex agreed that she would officially move in with Eddie at the beginning of the fall semester of their sophomore year. Eddie agreed that would be wise, but he insisted that Alex keep her things in the apartment for his reassurance.

Alex was happy when the semester ended. She was going to be at home with her mother for the summer and she felt like she would finally be able to breathe. Both of them would be working, so Alex hoped that would keep her busy enough to avoid Eddie without him realizing it. She needed time to heal and get her mind together for the upcoming school year when she would be staying with Eddie. She was definitely dreading it, but Alex felt as if there was nothing that could be done at this point. She decided to try and think positively about the future. She hoped that the next year couldn't possibly be as emotionally trying as the first year. But little did Alex know, she was in for a rude awakening.

13

*E*ddie decided that he wanted to be back in his apartment a few days before classes started for the fall semester. He told Alex that this would give them the chance to adjust to living together before all the stresses of college life began again. When Eddie came to pick Alex up, she greeted Eddie with a reluctant kiss on the cheek and got into the car. As Eddie put her bags into the trunk, she stared at him through the passenger door mirror. Her stomach had been in knots for weeks because she was dreading this move. Eddie had proven to be his wonderful self during the summer. He was thoughtful, caring, and charming, but his cheerful demeanor didn't fool Alex for a second. She couldn't shake the strong feeling that the monster would be back once they stepped back on campus.

Alex took a deep breath and exhaled slowly. She had been trying to convince herself all summer that she was making the right decision in moving in with Eddie. That wasn't easy to do with everyone in her life telling her that it was a bad idea. Alex's mother said that she was too young to be so serious about a boy, and her Uncle George was against it because he didn't believe in cohabitation before marriage. Tameka was suspicious of Eddie's motives behind the move since Alex told her about his infamous rants, and Alex's grandfather was just simply disappointed in her decision. They all said that they loved her and would be there for her if she needed them, but they couldn't possibly support her decision. After those conversations, Alex couldn't help but feel alone. She wanted to have at least one person on her side, but she couldn't blame them. She felt like it was a bad idea too.

When Eddie was finished, he got in the car and began to drive toward the highway. For the first couple of hours, they rode in silence. Alex wanted to talk, but she just couldn't find the words. She just couldn't believe that she was on her way back to campus and moving in with Eddie. Every second that passed gave Alex an increased sense of dread. She didn't want to be in this situation. During the entire summer break, she was trying to convince herself that she was moving in with Eddie to strengthen their relationship. But the reality was, she was doing it because she was scared that he would eventually leave her for someone else.

Alex had never been in a relationship where she was afraid that her boyfriend would leave her. She had always been so confident in her own self-worth that she figured if the guy didn't want to be with her, there was someone out there better for her who would. She never had to deal with anyone with a Dr. Jekyll/ Mr. Hyde personality either. Dealing with Eddie was definitely new territory for Alex and she still wasn't sure she wanted to stay in it.

When Eddie pulled up to his apartment complex, Alex helped move her things inside. While she unpacked her things and placed them around the apartment, Eddie thought it would be best to go over the "house rules" with Alex. At first, Alex was a little shocked that Eddie had come up with rules for her to live by. But after she thought about it, she realized that she was being silly for even thinking that she would have the freedoms she had without Eddie around. As Alex listened to the rules, she began to see a common theme in every rule—control. Eddie had to be in control of everything. Alex knew she was going to hate living with Eddie, and now she finally saw why. She reminded herself that she was moving in with Eddie because she wanted to repair their broken relationship and she reluctantly agreed to Eddie's rules.

Alex wanted to say that she would obey for now, but if he started in on his fanatical rants again, she was gone. But they had been down that road too many times before. She would say that if things didn't change, she would leave and he would tell her that she wasn't going anywhere. This time, Alex would need to prove that she wasn't bluffing.

When Alex finished unpacking her things, she told Eddie she was going to call it a night and go to bed. It was such a long day for Alex with the long drive and unpacking that she really didn't feel like doing anything else. Alex took a shower and went to lie down. She stared at the ceiling wondering about how the living situation with Eddie was going to turn out. As she turned over on her side and drifted off to sleep, she knew that only time would tell whether she was living with the love of her life or a monster.

14

Two months passed since Alex moved in with Eddie at the beginning of the fall semester of their sophomore year. When she was home for the summer, Alex tried to persuade herself to think positively about living with Eddie. But she was so glad she didn't succeed at that task. Eddie proved to be a true tyrant during the short period of time that Alex lived with him. She couldn't do anything without consulting Eddie first. He would monitor her phone calls and demand that he take her everywhere she needed to go. Once, Alex came home five minutes later than she estimated and that sent Eddie into a rage that ended in a broken table and holes in the wall the size of Eddie's fist. He would accuse her of cheating on him almost daily, despite the fact that he knew her every move, and he would criticize everything about her. If Eddie didn't like her outfit, she had to change and he would always talk about Alex's weight. Depending on what day of the week it was, she was either too fat or too skinny. Nothing pleased Eddie.

As time went on, things only got worse for Alex. Eddie's

unpredictable personality was beginning to affect her health. Her weight was up and down and she began to have severe migraines. She didn't sleep well at night because Eddie would always wake her up in the middle of the night to argue or demand sex. When Alex did sleep, she had nightmares. She would dream that Eddie was raping her or cheating on her; she even had a dream where Eddie was trying to kill her. Alex knew that she couldn't live in that situation anymore. She decided that it was time to leave Eddie.

One night in late October, Alex sat on the couch in Eddie's living room with a duffel bag beside her. She was waiting for Eddie to come home so that she could tell him that the relationship was over. With Eddie's history of violent outbursts, Alex had a feeling she should have left without him knowing and let him figure it out. But Alex ignored that feeling and decided to tell Eddie face to face. She looked at her watch and saw it was 7:00 p.m. Eddie would be back soon. Alex nervously twiddled her hands in her lap while she watched the door. She felt like her heart would beat out of her chest.

Finally, she heard the key in the door and saw the knob turn. She took a deep breath and waited for Eddie to walk in. When he did, he stopped cold when he saw Alex sitting on the couch.

"Is dinner ready?" he asked, closing the door.

"I didn't make you dinner tonight, Eddie."

"Why not?" Eddie asked, as if he already knew the answer to that question. Alex saw that he was eyeing her duffel bag, so she didn't say anything. She had prepared an entire speech for this moment. Now, she couldn't find the words, so she just stared at the floor.

"Let's try this again. Why…not?" he asked, enunciating and speaking more slowly.

"I was packing," Alex said softly, still starring at the floor.

"I don't remember you telling me anything about a trip."

"I'm not going on a trip, Eddie. I'm moving out."

"Moving out," Eddie said. He put down the items he brought in the apartment and leaned against the wall facing Alex. "You're joking."

"No, I'm not."

"Okay, Alex, I get it. Ha ha. Joke's on me. Now go put your bag in the room so we can get something to eat. I'm starving."

"Eddie, I'm serious. I'm moving out. I can't be in this relationship anymore."

"So you're breaking up with me?"

"Yes."

"I've told you before about making that threat."

"It's not a threat. It's reality."

"Look, I don't take threats very well, Alex, so you had better drop the charade before we have a problem."

"Good-bye, Eddie," Alex said, standing up and picking up her bag from the couch.

"So that's it? You're leaving me?"

"This shouldn't be a surprise to you, Eddie. You have some serious issues and I can't deal with them anymore."

"Issues? What issues?" Eddie asked, clearly confused.

"You're controlling and manipulative for starters. You are mean to me and you have these insane emotional outbursts that seem to come from nowhere."

"I can't believe you're really trying to leave me, Alex," Eddie said, as he began to pace. "After all the things I've done for you, you're going to stab me in the back like this? I've been nothing but good to you, Alex, so I know you aren't leaving me for the issues you say I have."

"Yea, the issues are why I'm leaving."

"Oh come on, Alex. Don't lie to me. Just tell me his name. I promise I won't be mad."

"There is no other guy, Eddie," Alex huffed.

"Sure there is. Why else would you be leaving me?"

"See, that's another issue right there. Accusing me of things I'm not doing and have never done, by the way. I'm leaving you because you treat me like a servant, not a girlfriend. You make demands instead of asking me to do something for you. You try to control my every move and you don't communicate with me; you yell at me. I'm done trying to make excuses for you so that I can convince myself to stay. I can no longer pretend that what you've been doing to me is okay. I have to leave."

"So you can't even be a woman about it and tell me the truth? Eddie yelled. "That's just like you, Alex. Woman up and tell me that you have a new boyfriend. You could at least have the decency to tell me to my face, so I don't have to find out from somebody else. So what's his name? Is it the basketball player? Is he good to you? Does he treat you like I do? Does he make love to you better than I do? What is it, Alex, tell me? Be a woman and tell me what's really going on!"

Alex shook her head and sighed as Eddie glared at her. He was never going to get it and she couldn't be his emotional punching bag anymore. She decided that it would be best not to say anything else, so she walked out the door. About ten minutes later, she knocked on Tameka's door and asked if she could crash there for a while. Alex wanted to tell Tameka why she needed to use her couch for a few days, but she couldn't find the words to tell her. She thought that the moment she left Eddie, she would feel like she was finally free. But she was distraught. Alex lay on the couch trying to fight the tears, but eventually there was nothing she could do to stop them.

Alex was battling conflicting emotions. She knew she still loved Eddie, but she just couldn't stay in a situation that was so unhealthy for her. Alex rolled over on her side in an effort to rest. Tomorrow would be a new day and she would have more energy to deal with her feelings.

15
_____

When Alex woke up, she realized it was morning. She sat up on the couch and grabbed her phone. When she saw what she had slept through, she was horrified. Alex had thirty-six missed calls, twelve text messages, and four voicemails since she left Eddie's apartment. The worst part about it; they were all from Eddie. As she scrolled through the missed calls and saw Eddie's name come up repeatedly, she could feel her throat tighten. Alex just couldn't understand what could possess him to act like that.

As she scrolled through the text messages, she was officially convinced that Eddie had some severe emotional problems. The first few text messages called Alex everything but a child of God, and continued to lash out about leaving Eddie for a guy that only existed in his mind. The next group of messages talked about how Eddie felt so betrayed and he kept asking how she could do this to him. Then the most recent text messages were messages of apology. He said that he was so sorry for the things that he had done to Alex and he couldn't live without her. He also said that he was in love with her and he would do what it takes to make it work.

Alex felt sick to her stomach. She didn't even want to check the voicemails, but she did anyway. Alex felt like it was important to figure out what was going through Eddie's head. The sequence of the voicemails was the same as the text messages. The first two were full of cursing, name-calling, and accusations about a boyfriend Alex didn't have. The third voicemail talked about how Alex betrayed him and how he had been so good to her. The last message bothered Alex; it actually sent chills down her spine.

It said, "Hey, Alex. This is my fourth attempt to contact you by voicemail and you still aren't answering your phone. You're probably out with your new boyfriend, so I will try to make this quick. I don't understand how you could do this to me. All I have done is love you and take care of you. Up until recently, I thought you loved me too, but I see that you got tired of lying in my bed and decided to lie in someone else's. I have been nothing but loyal to you, Alex. Anything you've asked for I have given to you, but that just wasn't good enough, was it? You found someone new and I get that. But I'm still in love with you, Alex. I always will be. I'm sorry that I lashed out at you. As a man, I should have just accepted your decision. Please call me back when you get this message. I want to talk. I love you. Bye."

After all the missed calls and rants through text message and voicemail, Eddie sounded too calm. Alex couldn't think of anything that would make him calm so suddenly. She knew that she had nothing to do with it. Alex sat on the couch for a minute and stared at her phone. She was debating on whether or not to call Eddie back. After about five minutes, Alex called Eddie back.

"Hey, Alex," he said, when he answered.

"Hey," Alex said.

"I'm glad you called back," Eddie said softly.

"I wasn't going to. Especially after all those missed calls last night."

"I'm sorry about that. I was just really upset about you leaving. I shouldn't have said the horrible things that I said. I'm really sorry."

"So what do you want, Eddie?" Alex asked, slightly irritated.

"What do I want? You mean, after all we have been through, we can't even be friends? I can't just call to see how you're doing?"

"No. I'm not interested in anymore contact with you."

"Wow," Eddie laughed. "You really hate me, don't you?"

"I don't hate you. I'm just done. I don't deserve to be treated badly and I won't be."

"So that's it, then?"

"That's it."

"Come on, Alex, don't do this. I love you. Please don't leave me. We can work it out. I promise we can."

"I'm not the one with the problem, you are. You sincerely need some help, Eddie."

"I just need you, Alex. Please just come home and let's make up. Let's work on us."

"No, Eddie. No more. I'm done. I'm coming over to get my things as soon as I get an apartment. Then after that, you won't hear from me again."

"Alex, please—"

Alex hung up the phone before Eddie could finish. She wasn't interested in making up this time. It just didn't seem worth it. She knew all too well what would happen if she went back to Eddie. He would be wonderful and charming for a little while, but then he would be right back to his cruel self. Alex wasn't interested in being part of whatever sick game Eddie was playing anymore. She was more than confident in her decision to leave Eddie, and she had high hopes for getting past this phase in her life.

16

*S*everal months passed since Alex broke up with Eddie and she was having the time of her life. She slept better at night and she was performing better than ever in her classes. She got to focus more on her extracurricular activities and she spent more time with her girlfriends. Life was looking good.

Alex was now living in her own one-bedroom apartment, which her family graciously helped her pay for. She was looking for a part-time job and she finally had her car with her. Eddie would try to contact her from time to time, but Alex was determined to keep her distance from him. The last thing she wanted was to get sucked in again by Eddie's charm.

One day, when Alex was walking out of the coffee shop with her chai tea, she ran into Eddie. She figured that enough time had passed for her to at least be cordial. They sat down at a table and talked. Alex thought it was a nice conversation. After about an hour, Alex said that she was going to leave. Eddie offered to walk her out to her car and so the two made their way out to the parking lot.

When they got to Alex's car, Eddie leaned in and kissed her. The kiss brought back all of Alex's feelings for Eddie and before she knew it, they were back in his apartment having sex. The entire experience felt like old times and how Alex wished that they could go back in time. But when it was over, Alex had to remind herself that Eddie wasn't that charming and wonderful man that everyone else knew him to be. Behind closed doors, he was cruel-hearted and controlling. She couldn't put herself back in that situation.

Alex rolled out of the bed and quickly threw her clothes on. She had to get out of Eddie's apartment.

"Where are you going, Alex?" Eddie asked.

"Home," Alex said, walking toward the door.

"Wait," Eddie said, getting out of the bed himself. "When can I see you again?"

"We aren't going to do this again, Eddie."

"Why not? You didn't enjoy it?"

"It's not that, Eddie. I just don't need you to get the wrong idea about what just happened here."

"Wrong idea?" Eddie asked. "What do you mean wrong idea?"

"This was a one-time thing, Eddie. It just happened. I didn't mean for it to. You kissed me and all these feelings came rushing back—"

"So wait a minute," Eddie interrupted. "Are you saying this doesn't mean we're back together?"

"Yes, that's what I'm saying."

"So you used me for sex?"

"I really wouldn't call it that, Eddie, I just—"

"This is unbelievable!" Eddie yelled. "I'm in here making love to you like we've finally made up and you were just trying to get off. That's cold."

"Well, I'm sorry you feel that way. I tried to explain my side but you won't listen, so I'm just going to go."

"Alex, wait!" Eddie said, grabbing her arm. "So you really don't want to be with me? And you really don't love me anymore? All of this meant nothing to you?"

"Eddie, stop! You're hurting me!" Alex said, trying to twist her arm out of Eddie's vice grip.

"Please, Alex. Just tell me you love me, and you want us back. Come back to me. I know we can work it out."

"There's nothing to work out," Alex said, finally freeing her arm.

"Please, Alex! Don't do this! I can't live without you," Eddie said, with tears streaming down his face. "I love you! Don't leave me!"

"Good-bye, Eddie." Alex turned and left Eddie's apartment. She hated that he was hurting, but she wasn't about to compromise her sanity and her health to be with him again. Alex felt like she needed an outlet so she drove to Tameka's apartment. When she got there, she told Tameka about everything that had been going on between her and Eddie since the beginning of their relationship. Tameka sat and listened to Alex in silence. She knew that Eddie had emotional episodes, but Alex never told her the whole story. She was shocked that Eddie would behave in the manner in which Alex described. Everyone on campus that knew him liked him. He was involved in everything and the women on campus wanted to be with him. He was attractive, charming, and charismatic. Eddie was the type of person who, once you talked to him, was difficult to dislike.

Just as Tameka opened her mouth to talk, Alex received a text message from Eddie before she could say anything. It said, "This is a good-bye text, Alex. I just want you to know that I love you and I never meant to hurt you. I can't live without you so I'm going to end my life. I hope that the rest of your life is blessed. Love, Eddie."

Alex felt her heart drop into her stomach. She ran out of Tameka's apartment dialing Eddie's number. He wasn't answering. When she got to his apartment, she started banging on the door and calling his name. After about five minutes, he answered the door.

"Came to say good-bye?" he asked, holding a bottle of pills. Alex tried to take the pills out of his hand, but he moved them out of her reach.

"Don't do this, Eddie," Alex said, eyeing the pill bottle.

"Don't do what, Alex? Love you? Need you? Yearn to be with you? Well, I'm sorry but I can't deal with the pain of losing you. So if you will excuse me, I have something I need to do." Eddie grabbed a bottle of whiskey off his kitchen table and headed to the bathroom.

"Eddie, don't do this!" Alex screamed. "You have so much to live for."

"Like what? I don't have you anymore."

"No, but you have family and you have friends. They wouldn't want you to kill yourself."

"They don't love me, Alex. They're just riding my coat tails because they know I'm going to be successful one day."

"That's not true."

"Sure, it is. But that won't matter anymore in about an hour."

"Eddie, please," Alex cried, tears streaming down her face. "Please don't do this."

"Why do you even care, Alex? You got what you wanted. You're doing everything you want to do."

"I care because I love you."

"You don't love me. You just don't want it on your conscience that I committed suicide because of you. Don't be selfish, Alex. Just let me do what I have to do."

"Eddie, no!" Alex said, grabbing his arm. "I know you don't want to do this."

"No, I don't. But what other choice do I have? I can't live without you, Alex. This way," he said, shaking the pill and whiskey bottles, "I don't have to."

"You don't have to do this, Eddie," Alex pleaded.

"Yes, I do."

"Please, Eddie, don't. I will do anything."

"Anything?" Eddie asked, with hope in his voice.

Alex hesitated. "Yes, anything," she said slowly.

"Okay then. Just live your life to the fullest and don't forget me."

"Eddie," Alex said, softly.

"What, Alex? Let me go so I can get this over with, okay?"

"Eddie, I'm begging you…"

"Don't beg. You're too good for that. Just remember that I loved you, Alexandria Stamford." Eddie went in the bathroom and closed the door. Alex's mind was racing. She didn't know what to do. It seemed like he made up his mind.

"Eddie, wait!" Alex yelled.

"What do you want?"he asked from behind the bathroom door.

"I will be your girlfriend again. Just don't kill yourself."

"You're just saying that now in the heat of the moment. You really don't mean it."

"Yes, I do. Let's get back together."

Eddie opened the door of the bathroom and walked out. "What's changed, Alex? You didn't want to be with me yesterday. Or for the past few months for that matter."

"I've always wanted to be with you, Eddie. I just can't deal with the Dr. Jekyll/Mr. Hyde thing you have going on in your head. It makes you appear emotionally disturbed."

"And I have apologized continually for that, Alex. All I wanted was one more chance to make it right. Was that really too much to ask?"

"No, I guess not," Alex said.

"So, do you really want to be with me? Honestly?"

"Yes," Alex said, already beginning to feel the resentment.

"Oh, Alex," Eddie said, embracing her. "I'm so glad we're back together. I don't know what I would've done without you." Eddie kissed Alex repeatedly. "I've missed you so much."

Alex lightly patted Eddie during the embrace and let out a huge sigh. She knew she didn't want to be with Eddie again. She just couldn't trust him. Alex planned to figure out a way to break it off again, when she felt like Eddie was a little more emotionally stable. But at this point, she was too afraid to. Eddie just proved to her that he was able to hit emotional lows that she never thought he was capable of. Alex felt like there was no way that she would be able to break up with him now.

Eddie wanted Alex to spend the night with him so that they could make their reunion official, but Alex wasn't interested. She made up an excuse about having a lot of studying to do and left.

As Alex drove back to Tameka's apartment, she tried to come to terms with what just happened in Eddie's apartment. No matter how much sense she tried to make of it, she still couldn't see Eddie's side of it. Maybe if the tables had been turned, she would have been in the same frame of mind. Even though she sincerely doubted it, realistically, there was no way to know. Alex's uncle always told her that you never know what you'll do until you get into certain situations, so you shouldn't assume that you would handle the situation better than the person in it. Maybe he was right, but Alex still had the hardest time grasping that concept when she felt like she was on the sane end of situation.

When Alex got back to Tameka's apartment, she was beginning to feel the fatigue of the day. She planned to run into the apartment, grab her things, and go to her own apartment. Alex walked into the apartment and Tameka was sitting on her couch. She sat down beside her and let out a heavy sigh.

"Anything you want to talk about?"Tameka asked, not making eye contact with Alex. She was always so good at knowing when something was wrong.

"He tried to commit suicide, Tameka."

Tameka nodded. She didn't seem surprised. "So where is he now? In the hospital?" she asked.

"No, he's at home," Alex said.

"So what happened?" Alex told her the entire story. Tameka just sighed and shook her head. "So you two are back together?"

"Yea," Alex said.

"That was a bad decision."

"You really don't waste any time, do you?"

"You know me. I get straight to the point."

"That's why I love you, T."

"Yea, well, I hope you still love me after I say what I have to say."

"Okay."

"Alex, I'm not gonna tell you what to do about Eddie and honestly, it's none of my business. But I really don't think it's the best relationship for you."

"I get that."

"No, I honestly don't think you do."

"What am I missing, then?"

"Eddie shows serious signs of being abusive, Alex."

"What?" Alex laughed. "No, I don't think that's his problem. He has never hit me."

"There are other forms of abuse, Alex."

"Like what?"

"Emotional and verbal. Eddie exhibits many of the signs of those types of abuse."

"Tameka, Eddie isn't abusive towards me. He just needs to work through some of his personal issues. Then he will be back to the man I fell in love with."

"That man doesn't exist, Alex. It's a façade. Now that he has shown his true colors, it will only get worse."

"Okay, since you're such an expert on abuse, tell me the abusive traits that Eddie has."

"When you were with Eddie, every move you made had to go through him. And when you did go somewhere, he had to be the one that took you and picked you up. He is excessively jealous because he is always accusin' you of cheatin' on him with boyfriends that you don't even have. He calls you constantly and leaves you threatening messages. You've told me that you had to walk on eggshells when you lived with him because his temper was unpredictable. He demanded sex even when you weren't willin' to give it to him. When he cheated on you, he blamed you for his indiscretion sayin' that if you made yourself more available to him, he wouldn't have cheated. He's called you unthinkable names and criticized everything you've done. And most recently, he has threatened to commit suicide since you didn't want to get back together with him. That's emotional abuse at its worst, Alex."

"How could you possibly know all this, Tameka?"

"My aunt was in an abusive relationship. It started out like yours. He was so good to her in the beginning. Then he started to change. The changes were so minute at first, that she brushed them off. Then he became controllin'. He wanted to move out of the state to a place where she had no family or friends. He wouldn't let her have a car and he wouldn't let her work. He criticized everything she did. Then the physical abuse started. He put her in the hospital four times, Alex."

"Wow, that's serious. How's she doing now?"

"She's dead, Alex."

"She's dead? You mean he—"

"Yea. He killed her. She got up the courage to leave him, so she found a way to save up a little money. You know, save the change she found around the house or keep a dollar or two after she bought the groceries. She stored the money in a shoebox in her closet because she thought that he would never look in her shoeboxes. But one day, he was gettin' dressed and accidentally knocked down the shoebox that had the money in it. He confronted her about the money, and she tried to lie about it. But he didn't believe her. So he beat her skull in with a hammer."

"Are you serious?"

"I have no reason to lie to you, Alex."

"I'm really sorry to hear about your aunt, Tameka."

"Thanks. Now maybe you see why I'm worried about you."

"All due respect, T, but I'm not your aunt."

"I know that, but I see all the same signs and I'm honestly afraid for your life."

"Eddie isn't going to kill me. And if he does become abusive, I will make sure I leave him."

"Then why not leave him now?"

"It would haunt me if he killed himself because of me."

"That's part of the control, Alex. You're not there because you want to be there. You're there because you're afraid he's gonna kill himself. That isn't a healthy situation to be in."

"I know, but I still love him. And in my heart, I want to be with him because I just know that he can be better."

"I love you, Alex. You're like a sister to me, so I won't lie to you. It's not going to get better. It's only going to get worse. I can't tell you what to do and I won't. You're an adult and you're gonna live your own life. But I need you to understand that Eddie doesn't have your best interests at heart."

"Thanks, Tameka," Alex said, giving Tameka a hug. "I understand that you're worried about me. But everything is going to be okay. I promise." Tameka nodded and walked into her room.

Alex grabbed her bag and went to her own apartment. The talk that she had with Tameka really shook her. She didn't know that there were different types of abuse. Now that she did know, it made her second guess her decision about being with Eddie. He really did have all the signs that Tameka was talking about. Alex shivered at the thought that Eddie could kill her if he thought she was going to leave, just like the man that killed Tameka's aunt. But Alex just couldn't believe that Eddie would ever hit her. Plus, she was a strong and independent woman. There was absolutely no way she would ever let a man put his hands on her and get away with it. Alex was confident that she had the situation with Eddie under control. She would in no way stay in a volatile relationship that could escalate to her own brutal murder.

*A*lmost two years passed since Eddie's suicide attempt, and Alex and Eddie were still together. They were now in their final year of college and Alex thought everything was going well. Eddie had been a dream since the suicide fiasco. It seemed as if he had returned to the sweet and caring man that Alex had fallen in love with. The couple rarely argued and Alex was happy that she felt free to do whatever she wanted without being afraid that Eddie would go off on her. He would have his angry moments from time to time, but they were in no way as bad as they had been before. For the first time in a long time, Alex had sincere hopes for the future.

After Alex agreed to get back together with Eddie, they sat down and had a long talk about their relationship. She told him that she would not be moving back in with him. She also told Eddie what she was willing to deal with and what she wasn't, and he agreed to all of her conditions. Alex was so proud of Eddie. He really seemed to be trying to make the relationship work.

About a year into Eddie's change, Alex informed Tameka

about Eddie's incredible transformation. She didn't buy it. She told Alex that his behavior was probably just the quiet before the storm. But Alex didn't agree with Tameka. It had been a year since that conversation and he was still wonderful. Tameka had to be misguided about her assumptions that Eddie was abusive. He was just going through a bad time in his life. Now that time was over and he and Alex could be in a healthy, happy relationship.

During the Christmas holiday, Alex decided that she wanted to spend some time with Eddie and his parents at their house in the country. Alex hadn't been out to that house since Eddie took her there to look at the stars on their first date. It was nice to see the property when someone was staying in it. The family brought in evergreen trees for the holidays and they lined the long driveway that led up to the house. The entire front yard was laced with Christmas lights that, despite the large amount, Alex thought was tastefully done. It snowed recently, so everything was covered in a thin blanket of snow and the pond behind the house was frozen solid.

The inside of the house was just as beautiful as the outside. There was garland hanging throughout the house and the air smelled of gingerbread. The Christmas tree was incredibly decorated and it sat beside a gigantic fireplace. Eddie went to put Alex's bags in one of the guest rooms while she sat in the living room. As she sat and waited for him to return, Eddie's mother walked into the living room with a plate of gingerbread cookies. "Hello, you must be Alex," Eddie's mother said, extending her free hand toward Alex.

"Yes, ma'am. It's nice to meet you," Alex said, shaking it.

"Have a cookie," she said, sitting the plate in front of Alex as she sat across from her.

"Thank you, Mrs. James," Alex said, picking up a cookie and taking a bite.

"Please, call me Melissa."

"I don't think I could," Alex said, nervously.

"Sure you could, dear," Melissa smiled.

"Okay, Mrs. Ja...I mean, Melissa."

"So it is nice to finally meet you, Alex. I can't believe that you've been with my son for practically four years and I'm just meeting you now."

"I can't believe it either."

"And where are you from again?"

"I'm from here."

"Interesting. You must be pretty special."

"Why is that?"

"Well, if my son waited all this time to bring you to see me, he probably wants to keep you around. He thinks I try to run his girlfriends away."

"Do you?"

"I do what I think is best," Melissa said, giving Alex an odd smile.

"Understandable," Alex said, trying to ignore the chills she got from Melissa's smile.

"Well, look, Alex, I'm going back in the kitchen to start dinner. It was nice meeting you and I look forward to spending more time with you."

"Likewise, Melissa."

Eddie's mother walked out of the room and left Alex alone. That was definitely an odd first conversation with Eddie's mother. She didn't seem to play when it came to her son. Alex just hoped that she would see the good in her and approve.

Eddie joined Alex in the living room shortly after Alex's conversation with his mother. She told him about it and he confirmed everything his mother said. Alex wasn't sure whether to be nervous or optimistic about this visit with Eddie's parents. If

Eddie's mother didn't like her by the end of the visit, it could be the end of her and Eddie's relationship. She felt like she was about to take a test and she had no idea how to study for it. Eddie saw that Alex began to look uncomfortable so he gave her a tour of the house, to put her mind at ease. By the end of the tour, Alex felt better. Eddie always had a way of making her feel good. Maybe the few days she would be staying with his family wouldn't be so bad after all.

efore Alex knew it, her time with Eddie and his parents was almost over. Her visit seemed so short and she actually had a lot of fun. They played several board games and Alex was surprised to find out how competitive everyone was. She watched some home videos with the family that showed Eddie when he was little; even back then, he had a ferocious temper. It was almost upsetting for Alex to see, but she reminded herself that Eddie wasn't like that anymore.

On the last night of Alex's visit, Eddie and his father, Sebastian James, went out to the store to pick up some things for the house. Eddie's mother requested that they go together because she wanted to talk to Alex. Eddie was reluctant to leave Alex alone with his mother, but after some strong persuasion from his mother, he left with his father.

Alex sat in the kitchen on a stool in front of the island. Eddie's mother stood on the opposite side of the island mixing some kind of batter. The kitchen was silent, except for Mrs. James's soft humming. She didn't even look at Alex. It was slightly unnerving for Alex to sit there when she knew that Eddie's mother wanted to talk to her. Finally, she stopped humming and said something. "Do you bake, honey?" she asked, still not looking up from her batter.

"No, I don't," Alex said, staring at her.

"I didn't either when I was younger. Never had the patience for it. Cooking made sense to me. Baking never did."

"So when did that change?"

"I met a boy when I was sixteen. He was a couple of years older than me and I remember I felt so special because I was dating an older man. From the moment I met him, I knew I wanted to marry him. And he loved sweets, so I taught myself how to bake and I would make him a dessert every week." Eddie's mother poured the batter into a Bundt pan and put it in the oven.

"That was nice."

"Yea. I was truly in love with him. No one could say anything negative about him if they expected me to believe it. I honestly thought we would last forever."

"So what happened?" Alex asked, curiously.

"We dated for about two years. At which point, the verbal abuse turned physical."

Alex's jaw dropped. "You were in an abusive relationship?"

"Yes. For four years."

"Oh my God."

"Yea, it was pretty bad. The abuse got worse and worse. I had numerous black eyes, cracked ribs, and fractured arms. I spent a lot of time in the hospital getting stitched up while trying to convince the hospital staff that I was just clumsy. But no one believed me. And I don't blame them. No one is that clumsy."

"Wow, that's terrible."

"You have no idea, honey. Toward the end, he threatened my life on a daily basis. And I got up every morning wondering if that day would be my last day on earth. Then two years after the physical abuse began, I found out I was pregnant. I was so terrified. I couldn't let the baby go through what I was going through. So I confided in a friend of mine and told her about what was going on in my relationship. She got me out the next day while he was at work. She helped me move across the country and get settled in a new town. I changed my name and everything about me so that he couldn't find me, because I knew if he found me, he would kill me. Eight months later, I had the baby. It was a little boy. He was eight pounds, nine ounces, and twenty-one inches long. I named him Edward Steven."

Alex frowned. "So, wait. Mr. James isn't Eddie's real father?"

"He isn't Eddie's biological father, but he is more of a man and a father than Eddie's biological father could have ever been."

"Does Eddie know?"

"No, he doesn't know. Sebastian and I met and got married before Eddie turned two. He doesn't remember a time when Sebastian wasn't around so that's the way I want to keep it," Eddie's mother said, looking at Alex sternly. Alex nodded to show she understood.

"So what happened to Eddie's biological father?"

"Last I heard, he got into another relationship a few years after I left and tried to treat her the same way he treated me. Only, she didn't take the abuse sitting down. After her first trip to the hospital, she went home and shot him to death."

Alex sat in silence for a moment drinking in all of the information. She was sure that Eddie's mother had a point.

"I'm sorry all of that happened to you, Melissa. But if you don't mind me asking, why are you telling me this story?"

"Eddie thinks I've given all of his girlfriends a hard time because I don't think that anyone is good enough for him. And actually, he is partially right."

"I'm sorry, I'm really not following."

"I have given all of his girlfriends a hard time, but it wasn't because I didn't like the girls. They were all really nice girls."

"Then why were you so hard on them?"

"Because I know my son, Alex. He is definitely his father's child. He can be so cruel and uncaring, that it's scary. I would ask you if you've seen that side of him, but I already know the answer. He can't keep his temper buried for very long."

"So you're hard on the girls because you feel like *they* can do better?"

"Yes."

"Then why are you taking a different approach with me?"

"Because you're the only one that's lasted this long and I can see how much you love him."

"I see."

"Look, Alex, I love Eddie. He is my heart and he always will be. But you seem like such a nice girl, so let me give you some advice. Don't get more serious than you already are about Eddie. There is no telling what that temper of his will lead him to do and I really don't want you to get hurt."

"Are you asking me to break up with your son, Melissa?" Alex asked with an appalled look on her face.

"I'm not telling you what to do at all. I'm not your mother and you're a grown woman. You're going to do what you want to do anyway. What I'm saying is, be careful."

"I can't believe we're even having this conversation. How could you bad mouth your own son?"

"Bad mouth? Wow, honey, you're more brainwashed than I thought. I can see where this conversation is headed so I'm going to drop it, but not before I finish speaking my peace. You know nothing about life, Alex. You are twenty-two years old and just as naïve as I was when I was your age. I would never bad mouth my son, okay? I told you the truth about him so that you could make a conscious decision about what you're getting into. Now you can believe me or not. It's entirely up to you. But one day, you will think back on this conversation and remember everything that I've told you. I just hope, by then, it's not too late." Eddie's mother turned to the stove and checked on her cake.

Alex sat in her chair fuming. She and Eddie were in love and wanted to be together. It was absolutely appalling that Melissa would say such negative things about him. Eddie had been nothing but amazing to Alex since the suicide incident. He was caring and loving. He did still have rants, but they were few and far between.

Alex couldn't understand why everyone had such terrible things to say about Eddie. He was better now. He actually changed for Alex so that they could be together. Alex wished she could prove to everyone in her life that she was right and they were wrong. She wanted to show her grandfather that his vibes from the beginning were incorrect. She wanted to show Tameka that Eddie was too gentle to be abusive, and she wanted to show Eddie's mother that she was seriously mistaken about her son.

Alex suddenly became determined to prove to everyone that Eddie wasn't as bad as they all thought. She was going to stick with the relationship until everyone else could see the good in him.

By the time Eddie and his father returned to the house, Alex had calmed down. When Eddie asked about the conversation with his mother, Alex told him they just had a little girl talk. She didn't want to tell Eddie about the conversation for fear of what he might do. Alex decided to turn in early that night so she excused herself and went to her room. As she lay in the bed, she began to have second thoughts about her determination to stay with Eddie. Several people were telling her that he was bad news, and if she hadn't been in love with him, she would have believed them. But this was Eddie. He was the man that she loved. Alex just couldn't convince herself that Eddie was the man that Tameka and Melissa described. Their relationship had just been going too well.

As Alex prepared to leave the next morning, she was overcome with a feeling of relief. She had a wonderful time during her stay with the Jameses, but after the conversation she had with Eddie's mother, Alex felt awkward being in her presence. She gave Melissa and Sebastian a hug good-bye and Eddie walked Alex outside. He said that he was glad she came over and he thought his parents really liked her. *Your dad does, but your mom doesn't,* Alex thought. She put on a smile for Eddie and nodded. After they kissed good-bye, Alex made her way home.

*a*lex adjusted her cap and gown as she walked into the Wellman Auditorium. She couldn't believe it was finally graduation day. Her four years at Pendleton seemed to fly by. Alex went to find the line for her graduating class. It was going to be a long day.

Alex's graduation ceremony was in the morning and Eddie's was being held later that afternoon. The families of both would attend each ceremony and then they would all attend a graduation party in the evening hosted by Sebastian and Melissa James. As Alex stood in line with the students in her major, she couldn't help but feel knots in her stomach. She was excited about graduating, but this was one of many days in her life that would be difficult to cope with. She tried to hold back her tears as she thought about the moment she would walk across the stage. Everyone would be cheering for her; everyone except her father and Brian. It had now been eight years since they died so tragically, and Alex was used to everyday life without them. But the special moments like graduations were particularly difficult to deal with.

The processional music began to play and Alex's line began to slowly move into the main area of the auditorium. When all of the graduates were seated, the ceremony began. Alex looked around the auditorium searching for her family, Eddie, and his family. Her family had been looking forward to this day since she was a small child sitting in her room trying to help her stuffed animals choose a career path. She couldn't see them in the mass of people, so she just looked ahead and focused on the speaker.

When the speaker finished her speech, the graduates began to line up to walk across the stage. After about thirty minutes of names being called, it was finally time for Alex's major. She walked up to the stage silently, praying that she did not trip and fall flat on her face as she walked up the stairs to shake the chancellor's hand. Then they called her name: Alexandria Michelle Stamford. As she walked across the stage, she saw her family, Eddie, and his family in the distance screaming and cheering for her. She smiled and waved, then walked off the stage. When the ceremony was over, Alex went to meet everyone. She was surprised to receive a couple of bouquets of flowers and several cards of congratulations. She gave everyone a hug and posed for pictures, then suggested that they all go to lunch together.

Everyone seemed to get along so well during lunch. They laughed and joked and told stories as if they had known each other for years. If anyone didn't know them, they would have thought that they were a big, happy family. When they left the restaurant, the two families separated so Eddie could get ready for his graduation ceremony. Since they had a couple of hours to kill, Alex's family went back to their apartment to drop off her gifts.

"So remind me again, why do we have to stay for Eddie's graduation?" Alex's grandfather asked, sitting in Alex's recliner.

"Dad, don't start," Alex's mother said to him taking a seat beside Alex.

"I'm just curious, Mickey. I don't know the boy and I don't get the best vibes from him."

"Yes, Dad. So you've said many times on the way up here."

"Well, if I had to keep saying it, clearly no one was listening to me."

"Grandpa, please," Alex chimed in.

"Look, Alex, we've talked about this. Your life is your life, but it won't stop me from saying what I want to say."

"I know," Alex said, rolling her eyes.

"So what's the deal with this graduation party we're supposed to attend after Eddie's graduation? Why are we invited to it?" her grandfather asked.

"Dad, we already told you in the car on the way up here," George said.

"Well, tell me again."

"It's not just a party for Eddie, it's a joint party," George said.

"Joint party?" Alex's grandfather asked, clearly confused.

"Yes, *joint party*," Michaela and George said in unison. They both looked at Alex's grandfather as if he knew why they were going to the party. Then, as if a light bulb went off in his head, he nodded knowingly.

"Right. Joint party," he said nodding.

"Is there something going on that I don't know about?" Alex asked, as she suspiciously observed the looks being traded between her mother, uncle, and grandfather.

"No, honey. We're just so excited to be here on your special day," Alex's mother said. "I'm so proud of you. Your father and brother would be, too."

She kissed Alex on the cheek and hugged her tightly. Alex's mother had come a long way since Alex left for school four years ago. She reconnected with some of the friends she lost touch with after the accident and she was hanging out with them. She was trying new hobbies and dating again. Alex was truly proud of her progress. She assumed it took her leaving home for her mother to finally decide that it was time to start living again.

Alex and her family talked for a little while longer and then made their way back to the auditorium to see Eddie's graduation. The ceremony was pretty similar to Alex's ceremony except the presenters were different. When the ceremony was over, everyone posed in pictures again. Then everyone left to get ready for the graduation party.

When Alex and her family arrived at the banquet hall the Jameses rented for the party, she was surprised to see such a large turnout. In addition to Eddie's family and friends, all of her friends and some of her relatives who said they couldn't make it for the ceremony were there. The hall was decorated in the school's colors, there was a DJ playing music, and there was food from a local catering company. Alex was impressed that the Jameses went through so much trouble for the graduation party. When Eddie's father was sure that everyone was present, he took the DJ's microphone and lifted his arms in the air to gain everyone's attention.

"Hello, family and friends!" he said cheerfully. "I'm so glad you all were able to make it to Alex and Eddie's graduation party!" Everyone in the room cheered. Mr. James waved his hands to silence everyone. He began again.

"When I'm done speaking, I hope that everyone will toast the graduates here today so please take a glass from the waiters as they come around. I just want to say how proud I am of my son for being a college graduate. It was a long, hard road but he made it. I'm also proud that he wants to follow in his old man's footsteps and study criminal law. He will attend law school in the fall and I wish him the best of luck in his studies."

More cheers. "I also want to say congratulations to Alex. She graduated today as well. Magna cum laude, I believe." Cheers erupted again. "She will be attending graduate school in the fall to pursue a degree in career counseling. She is a wonderful young lady that I have had the pleasure of meeting through my son. I believe she is an amazing addition to his life and I just want you to know that I consider you family," he said acknowledging Alex. "So here's to Eddie and Alex. May your lives and careers be blessed and successful. Cheers!"

"Cheers," everyone repeated as they lifted their glasses for the toast.

"Now," Mr. James said, "I'm going to ask our two guests of honor to come up and say something."

Alex shook her head in protest. She didn't plan on speaking in front of everyone. She just wanted to enjoy the party and mingle with everyone. Eddie took her hand and guided her up to the stage.

"Hi, everyone. Thanks for coming," Eddie said, taking the microphone from his father. "I'm glad you all could make it. I'm not really the type to make long speeches so I will get right to it." Alex glanced over at Eddie. She had no idea what he was doing. "I know that everyone in here knows why you've been invited up here and it's not just for our graduation."

Alex couldn't hide her confusion. She had no idea what Eddie was talking about. "All of you are here for this young lady beside me. I don't think it's a secret that I'm in love with her. She has been there with me through the good and the bad times. She has loved me despite my flaws and for that I will be eternally grateful."

Alex turned toward Eddie only to see him drop to one knee. She put her hands over her mouth as she felt the tears welling in her eyes. "I knew you were special from the moment I laid eyes on you," Eddie said. "After our first date, I knew that I wanted to spend the rest of my life with you. You are beautiful, intelligent, confident, and funny. No matter how bad my day is, just seeing your face makes it better. I feel like you are the other half of my heart, and now that I've found you, I'm complete. I don't think I can spend another day on this earth without you being my wife. Will you marry me?"

Eddie pulled a ring box out of his pocket and opened it. Alex stood and stared at the diamond ring. She was speechless. She had no idea Eddie was even thinking about marriage. Since she couldn't find her voice to accept his proposal, she nodded her answer. Eddie smiled as he grabbed Alex and kissed her. The entire room burst into cheers and applause for the newly engaged couple.

Alex couldn't believe it. She and Eddie were engaged. She was shocked that everyone in the room knew he was going to propose to her at their graduation party. He must have been working on his proposal for months with the help of his parents and her mom. Alex felt like she was floating. She went around the room showing off her ring to her friends and family. While she was doing that, she saw her grandfather pull Eddie off to a corner. They only spoke for a few seconds but by the look on Eddie's face, whatever her grandfather said rattled him.

When the party was over and everyone was on their way home, Alex decided to spend the night with Eddie. He didn't speak on the short ride over to his apartment, which concerned Alex after the exciting day they just had. When they settled in for the night, Alex asked Eddie about the conversation he had with her grandfather.

"What did my Grandpa say to you?" Alex asked, wondering if it had something to do with Eddie's silence.

"He said, 'I've got guns.'"

"Are you serious?"

"Yes."

"No way he said that."

"I was there, Alex. He said that."

"Why would he say something like that?"

"That's what I wanted to know. I asked him why he was telling me that and he said 'Simple. Treat my granddaughter right and you'll never see them. Hurt her, and you'll become well acquainted with them.'"

Alex was speechless. She had never known her grandfather to threaten anyone. "I'm sorry he said that to you, Eddie. That is completely out of his character."

"He really doesn't like me, does he?"

"He just has to get to know you," Alex said.

"You didn't answer my question."

"He's just really protective of me because I'm his favorite granddaughter," Alex said, trying to lighten the mood.

"You're his only granddaughter, Alex," Eddie said sternly.

"Yea, and I guess he feels like that gives him more reason to say what he said. I really am sorry. I had no idea he would say something like that."

"Don't worry about it, Alex. I don't blame him. How could he not want to be protective over someone as special as you?"

"Eddie, stop," Alex smiled.

"All right. It's been a long day so I'm going to call it a night. You coming?"

"Yea, I'm tired too."

Alex and Eddie went into the bedroom to lie down. Eddie went to sleep almost instantly while Alex lay awake staring at her ring. Her graduation/engagement day had been perfect, minus hearing about her grandfather's threat. Alex had never known him to confront one of her boyfriends, but then again, she wasn't as serious about them as she was about Eddie. Surely her grandfather had to get to know Eddie better so he could see his vibes were wrong. As Alex drifted off to sleep, she began to dream about her wedding plans.

20

*E*ddie and Alex decided to get married in August, a few weeks before they were supposed to begin their new schools. Alex spent the entire summer planning the wedding down to the last detail, and before she knew it, her big day had arrived. She put on her wedding dress and sat in one of the church classrooms with her bridesmaids. Then all of a sudden, Alex felt like she couldn't breathe. She told Tameka that she was going to get some air and excused herself from the room. Alex was going to step outside for a moment, but decided against it for fear of getting her dress dirty. Instead, she went to the church lounge and paced back and forth, eyeing the clock. The wedding was set to begin at two in the afternoon and she had fifteen minutes to go before it started.

Alex didn't think she had ever been more nervous than she was at that moment. Her stomach was in knots and she felt like she wanted to throw up. She couldn't wait to marry Eddie all summer, but now she was having second thoughts. She was concerned about being a good wife and making Eddie happy. Alex wanted to run away. She wondered if she could postpone the wedding for another week and think it over.

"There you are," Alex's mother said, walking into the lounge area. "What're you doing in here? Tameka told me that you left the classroom and she couldn't find you."

"I'm in the lounge," Alex said, sarcastically.

"I can see that," Alex's mother said, ignoring the sarcasm. "Is something wrong?"

"I don't know if I can do this, Mom. I thought I was ready, but I don't think I am. Is it too late to tell everyone to go home?"

"It depends. Do you really feel like you're making a mistake or are you just having cold feet?"

"I don't know, Mom. The thought of being with one person for the rest of my life is scary. How do I know he's the right one?"

"Sounds like you have cold feet, my dear."

"I really don't want to make a mistake, Mom."

"Do you love him?"

"Yes."

"Do you want to spend the rest of your life with him?"

"Yes."

"Do you want to give me a bunch of little grand babies?"

"Mom, stay on the subject please."

"Sorry. Just had to throw that out there," her mom chuckled. "If marrying Eddie feels right, then I say go for it. As long as you're both willing to make it work, you will have a successful marriage. Now, let's go make you Mrs. Alexandria James."

"Thanks, Mom," Alex said, hugging her mother.

"Anytime, babe."

Alex and her mother walked to the vestibule and got into their places in line. Alex stood beside her grandfather and watched as one by one, her mother, Eddie's mother and her bridesmaids left the vestibule to walk down the aisle. When everyone reached their place, the ushers closed the doors leading into the sanctuary. *This is it*, Alex thought taking a deep breath. She heard the traditional "Wedding March" begin to play and she suddenly felt a surge of confidence. She was ready. Alex looked up at her grandfather and nodded. The ushers opened the door and everyone stood.

As Alex walked down the aisle, she stared straight ahead. She was really doing it. She was walking toward her husband. She was about to be Mrs. Eddie James. By the time Alex made it to the altar, she was beaming. She knew she made the right decision. The ceremony went by smoothly and Alex was extremely happy about the outcome.

When Alex heard the words "you may salute your bride," she wanted to jump up and down with joy. This was the moment; the moment when she would officially become Mrs. Eddie James. Alex and Eddie kissed like they had never kissed before. When the kiss was over, Eddie put his arms around Alex as if to hug her.

He whispered in her ear, "Till death do us part, Alex. Remember that." He kissed Alex on her cheek and turned to face everyone in the church. Alex wasn't sure what to make of that statement. All she knew was that Eddie's words sent chills through her body. As she and Eddie exited the church, Alex could only hope that Eddie's repetition of that particular vow didn't mean that the monster she knew long ago was back and ready to wreak havoc.

21

*T*he first few months of married life proved to be more challenging than Alex thought they would be. Since she and Eddie were in a relationship as long as they were, she expected their transition into marriage to be smooth. She expected them to be excited to see each other every day when they came home. She also thought that household chores would be split between them and they would live in harmony. But tensions were high in the house. They both had crazy study and work schedules, which meant they hardly saw each other at all. When they were around each other, they communicated by arguing.

Eddie wanted Alex to keep the house clean and have a meal prepared for him every night when he got home. Alex wanted Eddie to be more responsible for the chores of the house because her schedule was just as crazy as his. The only thing they seemed to agree on was sex. It seemed like no matter how mad they were or how crazy their schedules became, they always had time for it.

Alex soon began to wonder if that was going to be the foundation of their marriage because it seemed like nothing else was going well.

As time went on, Alex began to see some positive changes in the marriage. She and Eddie were getting used to each other and their communication was improving. They were able to compromise on a schedule for household chores that benefited both of their busy lives. Living with Eddie proved to be an interesting learning experience for Alex. She noticed that he was very particular about his things. Everything had a specific place. If Alex moved something from the place he put it in, he would become angry. He also liked for things to be done a certain way and he made sure that Alex understood that.

One evening, Eddie came home in a sour mood. Alex didn't want to make him more upset by telling him he forgot to do the dishes so she decided to be pleasant.

"How was your day, babe?" Alex asked Eddie when he walked into the house.

"Is dinner ready?" Eddie asked as if he didn't hear the question.

"Yes," Alex said, slowly. "Did you have a bad day or something?"

"Can you go fix me a plate, Alex," he said, still ignoring Alex's question.

"Sure," Alex said walking into the kitchen to fix him a plate. After she warmed the food in the microwave, she brought the plate out for Eddie, who was already sitting at the table. She sat the plate in front of him and he took a bite.

"It's cold," he said, pushing the plate away.

"Really? I warmed it up in the microwave and I thought it was hot enough."

"You warmed it up?"

"Yes. I cooked a little earlier than usual so I could get some studying done."

"Alex, you know I want a hot meal when I come home."

"Okay, and the microwave can make it hot again. I'll just take it back in the kitchen and warm it up again." Alex quickly reached for the plate so she could put it back in the microwave, but Eddie grabbed her wrist before she could pick it up.

"So this is a joke to you?" he asked, twisting Alex's wrist.

"No, babe, I just—"

"You just, what?" Eddie interrupted. "You just don't want to make me happy? You just don't care if my needs are met? You just don't want to be a good wife? Honestly, Alex I'm getting fed up with your sorry excuses. When I come home, I want a hot meal. Not microwave hot, stove hot. Do you understand me?"

"Eddie, you're hurting me," Alex said, wincing from Eddie's grip.

"Do you understand?" Eddie repeated twisting Alex's wrist even harder.

"Yes," Alex managed to say through the pain.

"Good," Eddie said, letting go of Alex's wrist. "Now throw this away and make me a sandwich. And tomorrow, you'd better have my meal prepared the way I want it."

Alex hurried into the kitchen to make Eddie a sandwich. Her wrist was still throbbing. As she put the sandwich ingredients on the counter, she tried to fight the tears. Alex couldn't believe Eddie would hurt her in that manner. He had always been so gentle. Even in college when he would have his emotional outbursts, he wouldn't put his hands on her. The most he would do was punch holes into the walls. This was a side of Eddie that Alex had never seen before and she didn't like it. She decided that she would have to talk to Eddie about his behavior when he calmed down. She had to let him know that his behavior was not accept- able and she wasn't going to put up with it in their marriage.

Alex took the sandwich out to Eddie and sat down at the other end of the table to finish studying. When Eddie finished eating, he left the kitchen and walked out of the house without saying a word to Alex. She wanted to run after him to ask where he was going but after the incident they just had, she thought it best to leave Eddie alone.

When Alex finished studying, she looked at the clock and saw that it was after midnight. Eddie still wasn't home yet and Alex began to worry. She began to wonder if she should go out and look for him. She tried calling him, but his phone kept sending her to voicemail. Alex decided not to go out looking for him and to let him finish cooling off. She went into their bathroom to prepare to go to bed. As she was preparing to wash her face, she heard the front door open. Alex felt butterflies in her stomach. Eddie was back and Alex desperately hoped that he was in a better mood.

She heard him moving around in the kitchen before she heard his footsteps coming toward their bedroom. He walked into the bathroom and kissed Alex on her neck.

"I'm sorry," he said, handing her a small heating pad. Alex took it and laid it on the counter. She wasn't sure what to say to Eddie and she wasn't ready to forgive him yet. "You forgive me?" he asked, putting his arms around her waist.

"I don't know, Eddie. You really hurt me."

"I know and I was completely out of line. I had no right to twist your wrist around like I did."

"Why did you do it?"

"Today was a bad day and I guess I took it out on you. It won't happen again."

"Promise?"

"Promise."

"Good," Alex smiled. When she finished in the bathroom, Alex went to bed relieved. She was glad she and Eddie cleared up the whole situation. As she drifted off to sleep, she put the entire event from earlier out of her mind.

22

*A*lex walked into her bathroom one morning and pulled a washcloth and some makeup out of her vanity drawers. She gently washed her face and patted it dry. Then she stood in front of the mirror and stared at her reflection. She had a bruise on her shoulder, bruises around her neck and her left eye was blackened. Alex let out a heavy sigh and began to tend to her wounds. She thought about putting a little concealer on her shoulder, but decided against it when she remembered her shirt would cover the blemish. She covered the marks on her neck with the con- cealer since it was early September and it was still too warm for a scarf or turtleneck sweater. Alex did the best she could with her eye, which was half closed and swollen. She applied foundation all around her eye and used concealer to attempt to make her eye look as normal as possible. Her usual tricks weren't working for her eye this time. She would have to wear sunglasses.

Alex shuddered when she thought about how many tricks and excuses she had for covering up her bumps and bruises. It couldn't be normal to constantly research different techniques to appear normal to the outside world. She was always trying to hide something so no one would know what was happening behind closed doors. Eddie was a thriving law student with a somewhat famous father. She couldn't let the world know that he was hitting her.

When the abuse first started, Alex wasn't sure what to make of it. Eddie made it seem like it was a one-time thing. He got mad that his dinner wasn't hot from the oven and twisted her wrist around. He told her that he just had a bad day and he would never hurt her again. Alex believed him and forgave him.

About two weeks after the first incident, Eddie became upset because there were no fresh towels in the linen closet. He slapped Alex so hard across the face that her lip busted open. He later apologized to Alex for hitting her and bought her flowers. He promised not to do it again.

Since then, Alex received many bouquets of flowers, a gold necklace, two pairs of earrings, and a few pairs of shoes as apologies. She assumed they were supposed to make her forget about the black eyes, the bloody nose, the busted lips, the sprained wrists, and the many other bruises that appeared on her body after Eddie's tirades. She wondered what gift she would get for her new bruises. Alex went and sat on her bed. She couldn't stop the tears from flowing from her eyes.

Her marriage wasn't supposed to be like this. They were supposed to be happy and in love. But Alex was far from happy; she was terrified. She couldn't understand what she was doing wrong to make Eddie so angry with her. She really did try to be a loving and devoted wife, but nothing she did was good enough. He was always angry, always yelling, and always criticizing her. She felt like there was no way she could make Eddie happy.

As Alex began to get dressed, she thought about all of the things people said to her about Eddie before she got married. Her grandfather had bad vibes about Eddie since the day he met him.

Tameka was the first person to tell her that he was abusive and it was only going to get worse. Eddie's own mother told Alex that he was dangerous, but she didn't listen to anyone. She was too in love and too determined to prove to everyone that Eddie was not the man they described to her. But she was the only one being fooled. Everyone could see past Eddie's façade except her.

Alex felt like she was staying with Eddie because she had hoped he would go back to being the man she fell in love with. But as time went on, she began to see that she was only kidding herself. The man she fell in love with wasn't real. It was all just a charming ruse to lure Alex in. The man that abused her was the real Eddie. Alex wanted to leave Eddie, but she had become afraid of him. She couldn't help but shudder when she thought about what kind of scene he would make if she didn't come home one evening. Alex didn't want to have to face the kind of rage he would have once he forced her to come back home.

"Till death do us part, Alex. Remember that." Eddie's words rang in Alex's mind once again. She was beginning to see what he meant when he said those words. He knew he wouldn't have to pretend anymore. And as Alex feared then, his words meant exactly what he said; only death would get her out of her marriage. If anyone asked her before she got married if she thought Eddie would kill her, she would have laughed in their face. Now, Alex didn't know what to believe and she wasn't about to test Eddie and find out.

Alex walked toward the front door. As she passed through the living room, she saw Eddie sitting on the couch reading a book. She wanted to keep walking, but she decided to stop instead.

"Going somewhere?" Eddie asked, not looking up from his book.

"Yes, I'm going grocery shopping," Alex said quietly.

"Do you need money?" Eddie asked, still not looking up.

"No, I've got it," Alex said, anxious to get to the door.

Eddie put down his book and walked over to Alex. He put one arm around her waist and ran his fingers through her hair with his free hand.

"You know I love you, right?" he asked, still holding her.

"Yes," Alex said, not looking at him.

"And you know I hate it when I have to do this to you." Alex didn't say anything. She just nodded. "All you have to do is listen, Alex. That's it. Just do what I say and we can avoid things like this."

"Okay," Alex said.

"Good girl. Pick me up some orange juice while you're out."

"Sure, Eddie."

Eddie kissed Alex on her cheek and sat back down to continue reading his book. Alex put on her sunglasses and walked out of the door. She got into her car and sat there for a moment. *So now he isn't pretending to be sorry,* Alex thought. She shook her head and backed out of the driveway. She couldn't live in that situation anymore. It was time to go.

23

*F*or weeks after their first anniversary, Alex contemplated how she was going to tell Eddie she wanted a divorce. Every scenario that ran through her head didn't seem to end well. Alex was scared to even think about leaving because she thought Eddie might find out what she was planning. It seemed like he was always able to pick up on everything that was going on with her. Once, Alex pulled up to a gas station to get some gas and the attendant flirted with her. She thanked the attendant for his interest, but she did not return his advances.

As soon as she got home, Eddie asked her if there was something she needed to tell him. Alex said she didn't and Eddie called her a liar. He accused her of flirting with men when he wasn't around. Since then, Alex still couldn't figure out how he found out about the gas attendant. It was almost like he had her under surveillance.

From that moment on, Alex was extra careful about what she did. If a man would even so much as smile at her, she would break eye contact and quickly walk in the opposite direction. She was always looking over her shoulder to see if Eddie was watching her. Since Eddie always seemed to be a step ahead of her, she was even more nervous about planning to leave.

Eventually, Alex decided on a plan that she was comfortable with. She would leave on a Saturday when she was off and Eddie had to work. She would pack all of her things and go stay with her mother until she could get on her feet. Then she would file for divorce. Alex felt satisfied when she finalized her plan. All the time she spent thinking about it was making her queasy. She found it difficult to eat and all she wanted to do was sleep. Alex assumed her situation with Eddie was causing her symptoms so she put them in the back of her mind.

When her symptoms did not improve, Alex scheduled a doctor's appointment. The doctor conducted a pregnancy test and it concluded that Alex was pregnant. When she heard the news, she was inconsolable. She cried so hysterically that the doctor had to call in a nurse to help comfort her. Alex was miserable. In her mind, any chance she had of leaving Eddie was now out of the window.

The doctor advised Alex that if she didn't want to keep the baby, she did have options. But Alex knew she couldn't go through with any of her options. She couldn't get an abortion. If Eddie ever found out she was pregnant and didn't keep the baby, he would seriously hurt her. She couldn't give the baby up for adoption because Eddie wouldn't let her do that. She couldn't run away like Eddie's mother had from Eddie's biological father because Eddie would find her. Alex cried harder. There was no way out of her abusive relationship and now she was having a baby. She felt like she had written her own death warrant by getting pregnant.

Alex went home and sat on the couch. She didn't move for hours. The thought of having Eddie's baby left Alex almost catatonic with fear. When Eddie came home, it was dark outside and Alex was still sitting on the couch.

"Why are you sitting in the dark?" Eddie asked, turning on the overhead light in the living room.

"I forgot to turn it on," Alex said, staring at the wall.

"How do you forget to turn on a light when it's dark, Alex?" Alex shrugged and lay down on the couch. "What's wrong with you?" Eddie asked, sitting on the coffee table in front of the couch.

"I went to the doctor today."

"Why didn't you tell me you were going to the doctor?"

"Spur of the moment thing, Eddie."

"Well, next time you need to tell me where you're going. I don't care how spur of the moment it is."

"Okay."

"So why did you go to the doctor?"

"I haven't been feeling well lately."

"Okay, and what did they say?"

"I'm pregnant."

"You are?" Eddie asked smiling.

"Yes."

"How far along are you?"

"Six weeks."

"So that means the baby will come in June?"

"It's October, so yes. That sounds right."

"Oh, wow! I'm going to have a son!"

"They can't determine the sex of the baby yet, Eddie."

"Oh trust me, it's going to be a boy."

"Okay," Alex said, somewhat emotionless.

"Well, you just found out that you're having my baby! Why do you look so upset about it?"

"I'm not upset. I'm just tired, that's all." Alex lied. She really was upset about giving birth to Eddie's offspring, but there was no way she could tell him that.

"Well, of course you're tired," Eddie said. "You've had a long day. Why don't you go in our room and lie down and I will bring you something to eat."

"I'm really not that hungry. I'm a little nauseous."

"Nonsense. You can't stop eating now. You're eating for two and I won't let my baby starve. Food will make the nausea go away."

Eddie went into the kitchen to prepare something to eat for Alex and she made her way to the bedroom. Alex wasn't surprised that Eddie was forcing her to eat. Her being pregnant just gave him more reason to control her. She wouldn't be surprised if Eddie actually sat beside her until she ate every bite of food. He didn't seem to care that she was nauseous and would probably throw everything back up when she was finished. His ultimate goal was to prove that he was still in control.

Soon Eddie walked into the room with a tray. He brought Alex some soup, saltine crackers, and ginger ale in consideration of her queasiness. Alex was a little shocked at his gesture; he almost appeared caring. But Alex couldn't let his behavior fool her. She knew Eddie would continue to have rants as soon as his excitement from the baby wore off. Then she would become his punching bag all over again. She wished she could go through her pregnancy without being mistreated, but she wouldn't give Eddie any credit by assuming he would let up because she was carrying their child. Alex would just have to grit her teeth and bear it, and when the abuse got really bad, she would protect her stomach with all of her might.

*A*s Alex approached her due date, she began to feel sad that her pregnancy was almost over. To her surprise, Eddie treated her like a queen during her pregnancy. He waited on her hand and foot and he wasn't hitting her anymore. He painted and decorated the nursery. He also went on midnight food runs when Alex had a craving. It was as if he was an entirely different person. About halfway through her pregnancy, Alex found the courage to ask Eddie about his sudden change. He told Alex that she was pregnant and he refused to hurt his son. It was an odd response to Alex. She couldn't understand how he could have such respect and love for their child, but he wouldn't think twice about putting his hands on her.

Alex also felt as if Eddie stopped the abuse for appearances. He was all about maintaining a certain image. He didn't seem to mind Alex having to make up excuses for her daily bruises, but he assumed that a pregnant woman with bruises would raise more questions. Eddie was not going to ruin his image of being a wonderful husband and upstanding member of society. In Alex's mind, that was the real reason he was taking a break from the abuse. He was trying to hide the truth about what he was doing to Alex. Since Alex knew Eddie wouldn't hurt her as long as she was pregnant, she milked the situation for all it was worth. She enjoyed every second of being pampered because in the back of her mind, she knew the abuse would start again.

It was a Friday in mid-June when Alex went into labor. After about twenty hours of labor, she gave birth to a healthy baby boy who was seven pounds, 12 ounces, and twenty-one inches long. When Alex held him for the first time, her heart melted. She stared at him and cried as he silently stared back at her. She couldn't believe that she was finally a mommy. In that moment, it seemed like nothing else in the world mattered.

Eddie chose to name the baby after him. He said if his son had his name, maybe he would grow up to be just like his father. Alex shuddered at the thought of having to live with two Eddies in the house. She was determined to show her son that hitting women was not a positive attribute in a man. They brought baby Eddie home a couple days after he was born. As soon as Alex stepped into the house, she got a sick feeling in her stomach. She wasn't pregnant anymore which meant that Eddie would no longer hold back his rage. The only question on Alex's mind- *when would it begin again?* She knew she wouldn't be able to put an exact date on it, but she knew it was just a matter of time.

25

*F*or the first six weeks after Eddie Jr. was born, Eddie still treated Alex well. He didn't yell at her, hit her, or make demands from her. Alex assumed it was because he spent his free time with the baby. At the time, she hoped having the baby in the house would help Eddie remain calm and happy. But of course, it wouldn't. Alex nervously waited for the day when Eddie would return to his cruel self. When the day came, Alex was actually stunned by Eddie's viciousness. He proved to be even more malicious than he was before the baby was born. Alex assumed it was his way of making up for lost time. He made unrealistic demands that were impossible for Alex to accomplish. When she couldn't accomplish them, he beat her.

As time went on, Alex lost all of her freedom. She couldn't go anywhere without Eddie's approval, especially if she was taking the baby. Eddie made her quit school and her job to take care of him and the baby. He monitored her phone calls and emails and informed her that she had to cease contact with any male, who was not family. He put tracking devices in Alex's car and on her phone. And at the end of every day; he would check them to see where Alex went during the day and who she was talking to. He wanted the house spotless at all times, which Alex found extremely difficult to do with a new baby. If he came home and one thing was out of place, Alex was in trouble.

Alex was tired of being afraid of Eddie. She knew she had to get out of the marriage and take Eddie Jr. with her, even if it meant risking her life. She developed a plan that she believed would be the safest way to exit the relationship.

One day in January, Alex took Eddie Jr. to her mother's house for the night, and asked her if she would keep him so she could spend some time alone with Eddie. She didn't tell her mother that she would be back later in the evening with her belongings. She went back to her house and grabbed two large bags and began to throw clothes into them. Alex worked frantically and quickly so she could avoid running into Eddie. She didn't expect him home for hours, but she still worried that Eddie would discover her plan.

When Alex was finished, she dragged the bags toward the door. Then she ran back into the bedroom to grab some cash from Eddie's secret hiding place. She stuffed the money in her pockets and ran back to the bags. Just as she was picking them up, Eddie walked through the door. He saw Alex standing in front of him with the bags and he smiled cruelly. Alex stood frozen in fear. She did not return his smile.

"Funny story," he said, almost laughing. "I called your mom on the way over here to ask her if she would keep Eddie Jr. this weekend so I could take you on a romantic getaway. She tells me great minds think alike because you dropped off Eddie Jr. with her so you could plan a romantic evening for us tonight. I certainly didn't remember you telling me that you were going to be taking my son somewhere. And usually if I want sex, I have to come on to you, which means you wouldn't be planning a romantic evening."

Alex slowly lowered the bags and started inching away from Eddie. And with every step she took backward, he took a step forward. "So then," he continued, "I start to think 'something's wrong.' Guess my instincts were right, weren't they?"

Alex still didn't speak. She knew she was in trouble, so she looked around to find a way out. "So tell me something, Alex? Where are you going?" Eddie asked, no longer smiling.

"Nowhere," Alex said, still backing away nervously. She was hoping she would be able to lie her way out of the beating she knew was coming.

"Nowhere, huh? Then why do you have two bags by the door?"

"I just wanted to give some old clothes to Goodwill, that's all," Alex lied.

"Oh yea? Then why didn't you run it by me first? And why do you have money sticking out of your pockets? You don't need money to donate clothes."

Alex could see the rage in Eddie's eyes. She knew she couldn't lie about her escape attempt anymore. She ran around the side of the couch to try and get past Eddie as she headed toward the door. He grabbed her by the throat and pushed her into the wall. "So how about telling me the truth now," Eddie said, tightening his grip on Alex's neck.

"I can't breathe," Alex said, gasping for air.

"Good," Eddie said. "Maybe your lack of oxygen will give you an incentive to tell me the truth."

Alex struggled to breathe as tears ran down her face. She didn't want to tell Eddie the truth because she knew what would happen if she did. She looked into Eddie's eyes as he glared back at her. He wasn't going to let go until he got an answer, so Alex finally relented and gave Eddie what he wanted.

"I was leaving you," Alex said, barely getting out her words.

"So now the truth comes out," Eddie said, releasing Alex's neck.

She fell to the floor, grabbed her neck, and inhaled deeply, somewhat glad that she was able to breathe again. "Yes," Alex said once she caught her breath.

Eddie laughed sadistically. "You're a fool if you think I'm going to let you go anywhere, Alex. I've invested too much in this relationship for you to walk out on me now. I have loved you, taken care of you, given you a home and a son; and if you think you're going to leave and take my son with you, you are sadly mistaken. I told you long ago that I can't live without you and I've got news for you, I'm not going to. The only way out of this relationship is death. And I will kill you before I let you leave me. Do you understand what I'm saying to you?" Eddie asked, putting his hand around Alex's neck again and pulling her up to make her stand.

Alex nodded and managed a "yes" through Eddie's constantly tightening grip. He stared into Alex's eyes in silence for a moment, as if he was considering whether or not he should let her go. Then he said, "You know what? I really don't think you do."

He let go of Alex's neck and slapped her so hard she fell back to the floor. As she tried to crawl away, Eddie grabbed her legs and pulled her toward him. He kicked her in the stomach and in the ribs several times, which left Alex unable to move because of the pain. Then he bent down and began hitting her constantly. It felt as if every blow hurt worse than the last. While Eddie was hitting her, he kept saying, "You will never leave me! I'll kill you before you leave me!"

Alex lay on the floor in pain unable to block Eddie's blows. She knew she was about to die; there was no doubt in her mind. She could feel blood gushing from her nose and her mouth. Her entire body hurt terribly and she prayed that Eddie would just kill her so she wouldn't have to bear the pain any longer. As Alex endured hit after hit, she slowly began to lose consciousness. The last thing she remembered before she passed out was a blow to the back of the head.

26

*W*hen Alex woke up again, the first thing she saw through blurry eyes was Eddie staring back at her. As her eyes adjusted, she realized she was lying in the hospital. She tried to speak, but she couldn't open her mouth. She also tried to sit up only to realize she couldn't do that either, without pain surging through her body. She looked down at her left wrist and saw there was a cast on it. She assumed Eddie broke it. Eddie looked over his shoulder and gently patted Alex's hand. When he was sure no one had entered the room, he looked back at Alex with a cold glare.

"I don't have much time," Eddie said, quietly. "So here's what happened. You were a victim of a home invasion. The guy broke into the house while you were there and when he saw you, he attacked you. You fought back, but he was stronger than you. You don't know what he stole and you don't remember what he looked like. Got it?"

Alex stared at Eddie for a moment, before she nodded in agreement. There could be no way anyone would believe a robber

JESSICA R. GLASPIE

attacked her so brutally. Eddie walked out of the door calling for a doctor. A nurse walked into the room and checked Alex's vitals. "The doctor will be in shortly," she said, putting a notepad and a pen in Alex's good hand. Soon the doctor came in to see Alex. "Hello, Mrs. James," she said. "I'm Dr. Tonia Fields. I performed your surgery a few days ago."

"Surgery?" Alex wrote.

"Yes. Your jawbone was so badly damaged that we had to operate on it and wire it shut. It will heal best that way."

"What injuries do I have?" Alex wrote again.

"You had several head contusions and a fractured wrist. Your jawbone, nose, and three ribs were broken, and you have many bruises all over your body. When you got here, both of your eyes were swollen shut and you were missing a couple of teeth. Whoever did this to you had a lot of rage toward you, Mrs. James. Can you tell me what you remember about that day?"

Alex wrote down the story Eddie told her to tell if anyone asked. When she showed it to Dr. Fields, she read it and frowned. She looked suspiciously at Eddie, and then back at Alex. "Are you sure that's what happened, Mrs. James?" she asked. "I only ask because your injuries don't reflect the type of injuries you would get from a random attack. It looks more personal."

Alex gently shook her head and wrote, "No, it was a random home invasion." Dr. Fields looked at Alex for a moment in disbelief. She nodded and excused herself from the room. It seemed to Alex that she didn't believe the home invasion story either. When Eddie and Alex were alone again, they stared at each other in silence. Alex tried to break her gaze, but Eddie seemed to demand her attention with his glare. She felt as if she were staring into the eyes of a monster, because only a monster could do something so brutal to another human being. Alex had so many questions for Eddie, which she couldn't ask because her

138

mouth was wired shut. She stared down at the notepad trying to hold back tears.

Alex wondered how emotionally disturbed someone had to be to harm someone for not wanting to be with them. When Alex studied history in school, she only saw this kind of behavior from dictators and leaders of corrupt governments. The men who lead these regimes were controlling, manipulative, and deceptive using different kinds of abusive tactics to gain power. Alex felt like Eddie was the dictator of her life. She couldn't do anything without his permission or his money. When Alex tried to resist, he would criticize and abuse her until he got what he wanted. She realized she didn't have a husband; she had a tyrant. There were going to be no more plans of escape or anymore assumptions of freedom since she already tried to leave. Eddie would be watching her even more closely now. Alex looked up again to see Eddie still staring at her. He sat down at the end of the bed and sighed.

"It's a shame it had to come to this," he said, quietly.

Alex nodded.

"Maybe next time you will think twice about leaving me."

Alex nodded again.

"Your family should be back soon. I convinced them to go to lunch since you hadn't woken up yet. They'll be very happy to see you're awake. Do you remember the story that you're supposed to tell?"

Alex nodded and pointed to the notepad where she wrote the story down for the doctor.

"Good," Eddie said. "I'm leaving when your family gets back. And don't think because I'm gone you can tell the truth about what happened. If I find out that anyone knows the truth, I really will kill you next time. Consider this your first and final warning. Understood?"

Alex nodded solemnly. She had to decide what was more

important: staying with Eddie and enduring the abuse until he eventually killed her, or die trying to get out of the relationship. She didn't like the fact that all of her options ended in death, but it was the unfortunate circumstance of her life. She and Eddie sat in silence until Alex's family came back to the hospital. When they saw her, they gently hugged her and told her they were glad she was all right. Eddie announced he was leaving and kissed Alex on her forehead.

"I love you," Eddie said, staring deeply into Alex's eyes.

If Alex didn't know any better, she would have assumed he actually meant it. But she did know better, and she had the broken bones to prove it. She tried to force a smile, which was impossible, so Alex just nodded. When Eddie walked out of the door, she felt instant relief. She lay in bed staring at her mother, uncle, and grandfather as they talked amongst themselves about how they were so happy Alex was awake. Not long after Eddie left, there was a knock on Alex's door.

"Come in," George called out. A man in a suit walked in the room and introduced himself.

"Hello, everyone," he said. "My name is Detective Terrence Fields. I'm here to speak to Alex about the home invasion. Is this a good time?" Alex suddenly felt sick to her stomach. Someone called the police. She wanted to cry for her life. She knew if Eddie found out she was talking to a police detective, she would be as good as dead. She had to convince this detective of Eddie's home invasion story. She lifted up her good hand slightly and waved Detective Fields over to the bed. He walked over and handed her a computer.

"This is for you," he said. "I have quite a few questions and I know you may not be able to write them all out. There is a speaking program on the computer. When I ask you a question, just type your answer into this box," he said, pointing at the computer, "and press 'Enter.' Then it will say your answers for you. Is that all right?"

Alex nodded in agreement.

"Great," he said. "Could you give us a few moments alone, please?" he asked Alex's family.

Alex quickly typed into the computer and it said, "No, it's okay. They can stay."

"Okay," Detective Fields said, pulling out a small notepad to take notes. "What can you remember from the night of the home invasion?"

Alex typed Eddie's story into the computer. When it finished speaking, the detective nodded as if he was thinking.

"Your husband told me the exact same story a few nights ago when I interviewed him during your surgery."

"Okay," Alex typed," then what's the problem?"

"The problem is, I don't buy it, Mrs. James. When I got to your house, it was a mess and at first glance, I did think someone robbed you. But as I began to walk through your house, some things didn't add up."

"Things like what?" Alex typed.

"Like your cabinets and drawers were open as if the burglar were looking for something. The only things that were taken were a few pieces of jewelry. Most of your jewelry was still there and the box was closed. Now why would a burglar take the time to pick through your jewelry, take what he wanted, and close the box back? He didn't close anything else or steal anything else."

Alex typed, "I don't know. Maybe he only wanted the most expensive pieces."

"I considered that, too," Detective Fields said. "But then I saw you had a pair of emerald earrings still in the jewelry box. They have to be worth a fortune. Why didn't the burglar take them as well if he was so carefully picking through your jewelry?"

Alex stared at the detective. She slowly typed in her rebuttal. "Maybe they thought the earrings were fakes."

"I doubt that, Mrs. James. I know nothing about jewelry and even I could tell they're real." Alex couldn't deny that the earrings were real; they were a family heirloom.

"I'm not sure what to tell you. I don't know what was going through the burglar's mind," Alex typed.

"Okay then, maybe you can answer this. Why didn't he take anything else? You have an expensive sound system in your living room, pricey televisions, computers, and your husband has a couple of expensive watches. Why just take a few pieces of jewelry, Mrs. James?"

"I honestly don't know," Alex typed. She wasn't sure what to say to the detective. It sounded as suspicious to her as it did to him. Eddie had clearly done a horrible job of staging a home invasion. "You want to know what I think, Mrs. James?" Alex was afraid to ask, but she reluctantly nodded. "I think you know exactly what happened in your home."

"Wait a minute," Alex's mother said. "I know you aren't accusing my daughter of staging a robbery and getting beat up to make it seem real."

"No, ma'am, I'm only accusing her of lying about what has happened to her. One of her neighbors, who asked to remain anonymous, says she saw Mr. James come home about thirty minutes after Alex arrived. Then, here is the part that baffles me… our source says the police didn't show up for a couple of hours after he got home."

"Hold on," Alex's grandfather said angrily. "Are you suggesting that Eddie did this to her and staged a robbery to cover it up?"

"Yes, sir, that's what I believe," Detective Fields said.

"I'll kill him," Alex's grandfather said. "Where is he, Alex? Never mind, I'll find him."

Alex's heart began to race. She couldn't let her grandfather go around town looking for Eddie. It would make him really angry, and then Alex would really be in trouble.

"No no no!" Alex typed into the computer. "It really was a home invasion!"

"Don't lie to me, Alex," her grandfather yelled. "He hurt you, didn't he?"

"No, Grandpa. He didn't, I swear!" Alex typed.

"I don't believe you. I told you from the beginning I didn't get good vibes from him. Now we find out he's been abusing you!" Alex's grandfather said.

"Dad, calm down," Alex's mother said. "I believe Alex. She wouldn't lie about something this serious."

"Of course she would lie about something like this, Mickey. She's probably afraid of him."

"Dad, please," George chimed in. "Let's try to think rationally about this. Alex said he didn't do this to her and we have no reason to believe she is lying. We haven't seen any signs that Eddie may be abusive."

"That's because you can't see what goes on behind closed doors, George."

"Oh, and you can?"

"No, but think about it. We hardly ever see her anymore and that's probably because she is always at home trying to hide her bruises."

"Dad, you never see her because you're always traveling somewhere. We see Alex on a regular basis."

"And you never saw anything different about her? No bruises? No broken bones or black eyes?"

"Okay, that's enough," Alex's mother said, interrupting the conversation between George and her father. "Alex can speak for herself, so we're going to go outside and let the detective finish his questions."

"But Mickey—" Alex's grandfather started, but Michaela put up her hand to shush him.

"Let's go," she said. She walked out of the door and George and Alex's grandfather followed.

"Your family really loves you," Detective Fields said after the door closed.

"Yes, they do," Alex typed.

"Look, I'm going to level with you, Mrs. James. I know your home invasion wasn't real and I know your husband is the one who did this to you. I'm more than willing to take him to jail for what he's done to you, but in order to do that, I need you to tell me the truth. Is your husband abusing you?"

"No," Alex typed.

"I figured you'd say that. Most abused women do. Do you know why?" Alex shook her head. "They do it because they are afraid of what could happen when their significant other gets out of jail. They are afraid of getting beat up again."

Alex couldn't deny that she was afraid of Eddie, but she definitely wasn't going to confess her fear to the detective. If she did, it would be exactly like he said—Eddie would come back and beat her to death. Alex couldn't let Eddie go off to jail. She had to protect him with all her might because her very life depended on it.

"Mrs. James," Detective Fields continued, "if you were to tell me what really happened to you, I can promise you that your husband would go away for a long time."

"He wouldn't go to jail," Alex typed.

"Yes, ma'am, he would. Based on your injuries, we could probably charge him with attempted murder."

"Do you know who his father is? Who he is?" Alex typed. "Yes,

I do and that doesn't mean they are above the law. If he hurt you, he will serve his time like anyone else who abuses women."

Alex wanted to believe him, but she couldn't bring herself to tell him about Eddie. It was simply too much of a risk. She shook her head and pushed the computer away from her.

"So you have nothing to say?" Detective Fields asked.

Alex shook her head. Detective Fields let out a heavy sigh and picked up his computer. He laid his card on Alex's food tray and said, "If you ever want to talk or you find the courage to leave, give me a call. You're not alone, so don't ever feel like you don't have someone to confide in." Then he turned and walked out of the door.

Alex sat for a moment as she tried to take in everything that was going on. She concluded that everything in her life was going awry. She was in the hospital with broken bones and a wired jaw. Eddie would kill her if she tried to leave, and her grandfather wanted to kill him. The doctor didn't believe her story and neither did the detective. The abuse would get worse because she already tried to run once and now, people suspected Eddie of being abusive. Alex felt as if there was no way things were going to improve. There would be no more happiness in her life, and when she realized her truth, she cried.

27

*S*everal months passed since Eddie put Alex in the hospital and she was beginning to feel normal again. Her eyes weren't black and swollen anymore and the swelling was going down on her nose. The ribs Eddie broke were better and she recently got the cast off her wrist. Most of her bruises were gone and the wires were taken out of her jaw. She had her broken and missing teeth replaced after her jaw was fully healed. The only ailment that persisted was numbness in her lower lip and chin, but Alex decided not to let it bother her.

Healing was a difficult task for Alex. She couldn't do anything by herself and she was in constant pain. She was also afraid Eddie would get angry with her for not being able to do anything around the house and take it out on her already damaged body. However, she was surprised by Eddie's behavior. He took care of her and the baby, and he didn't hit her at all during her recovery. He also finished law school, began working with his father at his law firm and planned Eddie Jr.'s first birthday party without a single complaint or angry outburst.

Alex wondered why Eddie wasn't a wonderful husband all the time. He could be so caring and supportive and sweet; that was the Eddie she loved, not the monster who slept beside her every night. All of Eddie's abusive behaviors made Alex question her self-worth. She began to wonder what was wrong with her that made Eddie hit her. Eddie told her many times that she deserved the treatment she was getting because she wouldn't listen to him.

He would always tell her how she brought the beatings on herself because she refused to be obedient. Maybe Eddie would stop hitting her if she tried even harder to make him happy. Alex wasn't sure what to think. All she knew was almost everything she did upset Eddie. Maybe she did deserve the beatings, after all.

When Alex was fully healed, she saw how controlling Eddie could be. He installed surveillance cameras in the house so that he could monitor everything Alex did during the day. He sold her car and told her she was unable to drive unless he gave her permission to take his car. After saying that, he told her not to count on getting her driving privileges back. He took Alex's cell phone and told her she could only talk on the house phone. He told her that her telephone conversations would be restricted to one hour a day. If she wanted to see any of her friends and family, they would have to come to visit her. Alex felt as if she was on house arrest without the ankle bracelet. She wanted to make a sarcastic comment about Eddie putting bars on the windows too, but she changed her mind. She wasn't interested in taking a trip back to the hospital for mocking Eddie's rules.

After a few weeks of living under Eddie's new regime, Alex began to get cabin fever. She talked to Eddie about it and he agreed that she should have some fresh air. He told her he would give her twenty minutes a day to take Eddie Jr. for a walk around the block. He also said that before she left the house she would need to call him and tell him she was leaving. Then when she returned, she would need to call him back to let him know she was back at home. Eddie made a point to let Alex know this was her only chance to prove she was a loyal and devoted wife after her escape attempt. If she was even as much as a minute late, she would feel his wrath. Alex didn't want to lose the small amount of freedom Eddie was offering, so she agreed to his terms.

On her first walk, she discovered it would only take fifteen minutes to walk around her entire block. She figured she would take the extra five minutes to enjoy not being under surveillance. Alex chose to take her walk every afternoon around 4:00 p.m.

She would walk out of the house with Eddie Jr. in his stroller and leisurely walk past her neighbors' houses. When she got close to her home again, she saw an elderly woman who lived across the street working in her garden. At first, the woman would glance up at Alex and Eddie Jr. when they walked past, then go back to her gardening. But as time went on, she seemed to become more and more friendly. She introduced herself as Esther Cates and she always waved and said hello. As time went on, she would carry on small conversations with Alex about the weather and upcoming neighborhood events. Alex thought she was a nice lady and looked forward to their daily chats.

One afternoon as she approached her house, Alex noticed Esther standing out in front of her driveway waiting for her. She thought it was odd, because she usually walked over from her garden when she saw Alex approaching.

"Hi, Ms. Esther," Alex said, when she got closer to her. "Hello, sweetheart. How are you today?" Esther asked. smiling.

"I'm good."

"That's good, dear. I'm sorry to have stopped you on your walk, but I wanted to talk to you about something."

"Sure," Alex said, glancing at her watch. She had six minutes before she had to call Eddie.

"How is everything going at home, honey?"

Alex looked at Esther with a puzzled look on her face. It was an awfully personal question for someone she only spoke to casually. "What do you mean, Ms. Esther?"

"Oh, honey," she said, shaking her head, "I think you know what I'm talking about. Your situation with Eddie."

"Situation?" Alex asked before she realized what Esther was talking about. Esther was talking about Eddie being abusive. "So you're the anonymous neighbor who saw what happened?" Alex asked.

"Yes."

"All this time you've been talking to me, you've known about the incident and you didn't tell me? Why?"

"At first I was afraid to tell you. I was afraid you would tell your husband it was me who saw what happened."

"Then why are you confessing now?"

"Because I can no longer be silent when it comes to a life or death situation."

"Ms. Esther, I think you're a little out of line."

"I know your life is none of my business, but I had to talk to you about it. It really bothers me."

Alex looked at her watch. She had four minutes left. "Okay, Ms. Esther. Tell me what's on your mind."

"I saw you when the EMTs wheeled you out of your house on a gurney. I knew you were still alive because you weren't in a body bag. But I know that it was only by the grace of God that you were alive. I can't imagine the amount of rage it would take for someone to do what your husband did to you. You should have died that day. But you're still here. You have been given a second chance to live. So live your life and leave this man. You don't deserve to be abused. No one does."

Alex wiped tears from her eyes. She never thought she would

have to have this conversation with anyone. "I can't leave, Ms. Esther. He will kill me if I leave," Alex said quietly.

"He's going to kill you if you stay, honey."

"I have no place to go."

"Well, if you don't have family, I will help you get out."

"I have family, but he would find me there. He would make me come back."

"He can't make you do anything you don't want to do."

"Yes, he can, Ms. Esther. You don't know him like I do."

"I don't have to know him to know the type of man he is. He only has power over you if you let him. He can only control you if you let him. He can only hit you if you let him."

"That's not true."

"Yes, it is. You have to get out before it's too late, honey. If not for yourself, then do it for your son."

Alex looked at her watch. Two minutes before she was in trouble. "Thanks for the chat, Ms. Esther, but I'm afraid I have to go."

"I understand. Just think about what I said."

Alex nodded and walked toward her house. She didn't know what to think. She knew she should leave Eddie, but she couldn't risk her life doing it. She was just too afraid of having to face Eddie's rage. Alex looked at her watch and saw that she only had seconds to call Eddie. She pulled Eddie Jr. out of the stroller and rushed into the house to make her phone call. She was relieved when Eddie didn't answer, so she left him a message. Alex's heart was beating wildly in her chest. She couldn't believe how close she came to losing what little freedom she had. It all could have been lost over a conversation that wouldn't help her anyway.

It was almost laughable to Alex how so many people could tell her to leave Eddie as if it were so simple. She assumed it had to be the mindset of someone who had never been in an abusive relationship. It's easy to tell someone how you would handle a situation when you aren't the person in it. But the truth of the matter was, no one really knew the extent of what she was going through.

They did not have to live in a home where cameras watched their every move. They could go where they pleased and not have to worry about someone getting angry and hitting them. No one else had to be constantly controlled and criticized and called horrible names. And not one of the people who offered to help received almost daily threats on their lives. Alex was sure none of them were going through what she was going through. If they were, they would understand that it was impossible for her to leave.

Alex hated herself for constantly giving Eddie the benefit of the doubt over the years. She would always tell Tameka that he was only going through a phase or he was just stressed from classes. She was so in love that she couldn't see what was right in front of her face. She was well aware that when someone loves you, they shouldn't hurt you in any way. But even though Alex knew this, she wouldn't leave Eddie. Her son needed a mother and he wouldn't have one if she tried to leave again.

28

A few weeks after Alex and Eddie's third wedding anniversary, Eddie decided he wanted to have dinner with his parents. So one evening in early September, they left Eddie Jr. with Alex's mom and they made their way over to Eddie's parents' house. Eddie's parents greeted the couple warmly and they all sat down to a nice dinner. Alex smiled and pretended like everything was wonderful between her and Eddie. She laughed and put on a charming façade that could have fooled anyone. Alex had to admit, she knew how to hide the signs of her tumultuous home life. She loathed herself for knowing how to play this game so well, but she knew it was necessary for her safety. Eddie was all about image. If Alex acted as if anything was wrong, she knew what to expect when she got home.

Alex remembered all too well the first time she acted as if something was wrong at home. Her action was completely involuntary, but Eddie accused her of trying to show people she was afraid of him. It happened around the time Eddie first started physically abusing Alex. They stopped at a store on their way home one evening to buy some household items. Eddie went to the aisle that housed the toilet paper only to see the brand he liked was on the top shelf. When he reached up to get it, Alex flinched as she had any time Eddie raised his hand around her. He looked at her and said, "Don't do that. People in here will think I hit you."

The truth was, Eddie was hitting her and his abuse had gotten worse since then. Alex looked at Eddie from her seat at the dinner table and wondered if anyone could tell he was an abuser. She wondered if anyone could see past his sweet smile and charming personality to the cold, uncaring monster he really was. Alex knew firsthand how difficult it was to see past Eddie's charm. She couldn't see past it for years, despite the obvious signs that something was clearly wrong with him. The entire time he would have emotional outbursts and insult her and disrespect her, she would make up excuses for his behavior. She would defend him and lie for him to explain his behavior. She did all of that because she loved him; only to learn later that love doesn't work in a deceptive and hurtful manner.

Alex knew she was the only person, other than Eddie's mother, who saw Eddie's dark side, and even she didn't know the full story. Everyone else could only see the charm. He was loved throughout their neighborhood and their community. He was thought to be a prize in his father's law firm. He was an excellent provider and wonderful father. From the outside looking in, he was any woman's dream. Even if she found the courage to leave, no one would believe she wasn't the cause of their demise. People wouldn't believe that he was abusing and terrorizing her. She would be a pariah in her own city. The rumor mill would probably say she was a tramp and she left Eddie for another man. No one would be willing to accept the truth that their beloved friend, coworker, and neighbor was an abuser. Alex suddenly became sad, but she kept her composure. She wouldn't get beat up tonight for giving any inclination that something was wrong. Maybe in time, Eddie would be exposed for who he really was. After all, her Uncle George would always tell her that what's done in the dark always shows up in the light.

When dinner was over, Eddie and Sebastian went to check out Sebastian's new car, which left Alex alone with Eddie's mother. The last time they were alone together, Melissa told Alex that her son had a nasty temper and it was something she should consider before taking the relationship further. They spent a lot of time together since then, but they were never alone in the same room together, which relieved Alex since she felt awkward every time she was around her.

At the time, Alex assumed his mother just didn't like her and was trying to keep her away from her son. Now that she knew the truth, she knew it was only a concerned mother giving a vital warning about her son. Alex and Melissa sat at the table in silence for a while. Then finally, Melissa broke the silence.

"Help me clear the table, Alex," she said, picking up the plates and glasses.

"Sure," Alex said, picking up the things Melissa left. She followed her into the kitchen and helped her load the dishwasher. Then Alex sat on a stool as Melissa began to gather ingredients for oatmeal raisin cookies.

"Have you learned how to bake yet?" Melissa asked, measuring her ingredients.

"Yes I have. Eddie wants something sweet from time to time, so I had to learn."

"I figured you would. I find it interesting, though, that you didn't come to me when you were learning. I would've helped you."

"I felt weird around you since the conversation we had before Eddie and I got married. So I decided to learn on my own."

"Right. I remember that conversation. You seemed upset with me when it was over."

"I was. I thought you were subtly telling me to stay away from your son."

"Well, what do you think of the conversation now?"

Alex hesitated before she answered. She wasn't sure what to say. She didn't want to come right out and say "you were right, Eddie's abusive." If Eddie found out she was confessing, especially to his mother, he would surely kill her.

"I think," Alex said, slowly, "that you were just trying to help me out by warning me."

Melissa looked at Alex for a second and nodded. "Yes, that's true. I hoped you would take my advice and let him go ,but you decided to marry him."

"So, now you're saying I shouldn't have married him?"

"I think we both know you shouldn't have married him, dear."

"You know what, Melissa? You're being very disrespectful right now."

"Oh, come on, Alex. Don't assume I'm naïve to what's been going on with you. Why don't you tell me the truth?"

"Nothing is going on, Melissa," Alex said defensively.

"That lie may work with other people, but I know better. Eddie's abusing you, isn't he?"

"No, he isn't," Alex lied.

"Now you're lying to a formerly abused woman. I know the signs. No matter what front you put on or how much you lie, I can see the fear in your eyes when he's around you. I know every trick there is to cover the wounds from abuse and I've seen you use a few. I'm no fool. Just tell me the truth. Is my son abusing you?"

"No," Alex insisted.

"Do you want to know why I didn't come see you in the hospital?" Melissa asked, trying a different approach.

"Sure."

"I didn't want to face the reality that my son probably put you there."

"Well, he didn't," Alex said.

"Oh, honey. I don't know who you're trying to convince. Me or yourself. Gatesville may not be a small town, but people talk like it is. I heard what happened to you and if the rumors were true, you should have died."

"So other people know about it?"

"Yes, but they believe you were robbed. I know better though. Look, Alex. I'm not accusing you of anything and I don't want you to get hurt by anyone. I don't care if he is my son, no woman deserves for a man to put his hands on her. So please don't sit there and insult me by lying to me. Tell me the truth, please."

Alex cried silently. She knew she couldn't lie anymore. "Yes, he is abusing me," Alex whispered.

"I was afraid of that. Tell me what we can do to get you out."

"I can't leave, Melissa. He'll kill me."

"He'll kill you if you stay."

"That's what Ms. Esther said, too."

"Who is she?"

"The woman who lives across the street from us. She saw what happened to me that day."

"What did happen?"

"I dropped off Eddie Jr. with my mom so I could pack some things and leave Eddie. I went into the house, packed some things, and tried to leave. That's when Eddie caught me and beat me up. In the hospital, he told me to tell everyone that it was a home invasion. A police detective interviewed me and he didn't believe me. He said the evidence didn't add up to a home invasion. Later, the neighbor, who at the time wanted to remain anonymous, told me she saw Eddie's car pull into the driveway about thirty minutes after I got there. But the police didn't get to our house for a couple of hours after that. She saw EMTs roll me out in a gurney and I guess she put two and two together."

"So he almost killed you and staged a burglary?"

"Yes."

Melissa shook her head in disappointment. "I'll kill him."

"No, Melissa! Don't do that! He will know I told you about him."

"I could care less what he knows. My only concern is with you and my grandson. You need to get out of this situation."

"I know."

"So when do you want to do it?"

"I'll let you know."

"Alex, this isn't a casual conversation where we're discussing when we're going to meet for lunch. We're talking about your life."

"I know that, but right now I can't leave. I just can't."

"Why? Because you're afraid?" Alex didn't answer. "Guns protect scared people, Alex."

"No, I don't like guns," Alex said.

"Look, I know I can't force you to leave. You will only go when you find the courage to say you're not going to take any more abuse. But don't let your method of leaving be your soul leaving your body."

"I understand."

"I can only hope so," Melissa said, putting lumps of cookie dough on a baking sheet. "When you're ready to leave, give me a call and I will help you."

"You're not afraid of what Eddie might do?"

"I'm not afraid of anybody, and Eddie wouldn't dare put his hands on me. I would kill him."

"You wouldn't really kill your own son, Melissa."

Melissa put the baking sheet into the oven. "Come with me," she said, walking out of the kitchen. She walked into the study and opened a drawer in an antique mahogany desk. She pulled out a .38-caliber handgun and showed it to Alex.

"Like I said in the kitchen, I'm not afraid of anyone. I learned my lesson about abusive men twenty-six years ago. They don't play games and neither do I. No man will ever put his hands on me again, without risking his own life. I have one of these hidden upstairs as well. Don't let your fear stop you from doing what's right, Alex. No man has any right to hurt you; not even my own son. So like I said before, when you're ready to get out. You call me and I will get you out."

"Does Sebastian know you have these guns?"

"It doesn't matter whether he knows or not. He'll come into contact with one of them too if he decides to put his hands on me."

"Wow, Melissa, maybe you should go to counseling for what happened to you because you seem anxious to shoot somebody."

"Oh honey," Melissa said, shaking her head. "I went to counseling and I would never be anxious to kill. But what you don't realize about abusive men is when it comes down to your life or his, they will kill you if you don't kill them first. They are volatile and calculating, so you need to be ready to defend yourself if your life depends on it."

"But he's your son, Melissa."

"I know. And it saddens my heart that he has turned into the man his father was. Sebastian and I raised him so much better than this. We taught him to respect women. But I guess you can't override a person's DNA no matter how hard you try."

"I don't know what to say, Melissa."

"Say you'll leave. Say you'll come up with an exit plan so we can get you out of that house. Say you'll come stay with me and Sebastian if you're too afraid to go anywhere else. We will protect you."

"Eddie is your son. He would come around because you're his parents. I couldn't stay here even if I did decide to leave."

"Well then, we'll help you get a job and help you get on your feet in another city. I'll make sure Eddie doesn't bother you."

"Eddie would still bother me and you know it. We have a child together which means I'm stuck with him for life."

"Having a child with someone doesn't mean you have to be with them, especially if they're mistreating you."

"Thanks for all of your advice and your offer to help, but I really can't accept it, Melissa."

"I understand. I'm Eddie's mother and you see an obvious conflict of interest and I understand you wouldn't feel safe. But promise me this, if you don't accept my help, accept someone else's. Don't tarry on this decision. Leave Eddie and do it soon."

Alex nodded."Thanks, Melissa." She gave Melissa a quick hug and walked with her back to the kitchen. Sebastian and Eddie came into the kitchen as Melissa took the cookies out of the oven.

"You two were gone a long time," Melissa said.

"Yea, babe, sorry about that. I just had to show Eddie how the car drives," Sebastian said, kissing Melissa on the cheek.

"It's okay, I wasn't worried," Melissa smiled.

"What's wrong with you?" Eddie asked Alex, before he took a bite of a cookie.

"What do you mean?" she asked. nervously.

"Your eyes are bloodshot," he said, staring intently.

"I'm just really tired," Alex said, forcing a yawn. She hoped Eddie would believe her story. She didn't want him to know she had been crying. Luckily for her, her eyes would always become red when she was tired.

"Okay," he said, as if he was satisfied with her answer. "Mom, are these cookies for me?" Eddie asked Melissa.

"Of course, baby," she said, putting the cookies into a container.

"Great," Eddie said. "Well, it's getting late and my beautiful wife is tired so we're going to head out."

"Okay, drive safe," Melissa said, hugging Eddie, then hugging Alex. Alex hugged Sebastian and she and Eddie left.

Alex spent the entire ride home thinking about her conversation with Melissa. She couldn't believe she would take her side over her own son. It was admirable that she cared so much, but it was still too risky for Alex to consider leaving. She wouldn't leave Eddie. She was too afraid to leave him. She would have to ride it out and pray for the best. Hopefully one day, she would find the courage and the strength to leave Eddie.

he next few months were the most peaceful months Alex experienced since she was pregnant. Eddie was working on a big case at the law firm, which meant he spent long hours at the office. It seemed he only came home to sleep and change clothes so when he was home, she stayed out of his way. Alex enjoyed being alone. She finally felt as if she had some breathing room. For the first time in a long time, she wasn't looking over her shoulder, waiting for the next beating. That must have been how women who weren't abused felt —safe and free.

Alex knew better than to get used to being comfortable in her home, though. As long as Alex had the house clean and a meal prepared when he walked into the house, Eddie wouldn't say anything to her. But Eddie's case would be over eventually and everything would be back to normal. Soon he would be back to slapping Alex for not having the towels folded in the way he liked or trying to strangle her because she made a comment he didn't like. So Alex made sure she relished every minute of her abuse-free time.

When Eddie's big case was over, he wanted to go out and cele-brate his victory with Alex. She didn't want to go, but she agreed in order to please Eddie. Alex was exhausted. Eddie Jr. had a bad cold so she spent the day taking care of him and the night trying to get him to sleep. Alex got dressed and got the baby ready. While she was putting on her makeup, she couldn't help but dwell on the moment. It was times like this that made her resent Eddie. He knew Eddie Jr. was sick and that she was exhausted, but none of it mattered to him. She had to do what he said, despite how she felt, or face the consequences. It always made her regret the day she married him. She finished getting ready and put a few extra things into Eddie Jr.'s diaper bag.

They dropped the baby off at Eddie's parents' house and made their way to the restaurant. When they got there, Alex was surprised to learn some of Eddie's colleagues and their wives were joining them for dinner. She tried to perk up and put on a smile, so she could make a good impression. She shuddered to think what would happen to her if anyone noticed she was tired. Eddie would have a conniption when they got home. Dinner was full of laughter, playful banter, and wine. Alex decided not to drink anything when she saw how fast Eddie was filling and refilling his wine glass.

When it was time to leave the restaurant, Alex convinced Eddie to give her the keys. He was too drunk to drive home. On the way, she called Melissa and asked if she could keep Eddie Jr. for the night so she could take care of Eddie. When they got home, Alex helped Eddie out of the car and they walked into the house. They went into the bedroom and Eddie sat down on the bed. He took off his clothes while he stared at Alex.

"You know you looked really sexy tonight, right?" he said, eyeing Alex seductively.

"I just wore what you asked me to wear," Alex said, sighing.

"I know, and you looked good in it," he said.

"Thanks," Alex said.

"Baby, come here," Eddie said, standing up and walking toward Alex.

"No, Eddie. Let's just go to bed. Can we just go to bed tonight, please?"

"Why, baby?" Eddie asked while he put his arms around Alex's waist and began to kiss her neck.

"Because you're drunk and I'm exhausted."

"But I want you, babe."

"I'm not in the mood, Eddie. I'm tired."

"Please, baby," Eddie said. "I need you. It's been such a long time since I've made love to you."

"I know, Eddie. Tomorrow, I promise."

"Not tomorrow, tonight."

"No, Eddie. Not tonight."

"Oh, come on, baby," Eddie said, trying to unzip Alex's dress.

"Eddie, I really don't have the energy."

"You don't have to do anything. Just lay there."

"No, Eddie, I'm serious. Can we please just go to bed?"

"You know I don't like hearing no, Alex," Eddie said, finally getting Alex's dress off.

"I know," Alex said, nervously.

"Then stop being stubborn and give me what I want." He put a hand between Alex's thighs, but Alex pushed it away before she realized what she was doing. Her involuntary action infuriated Eddie so much that he slapped Alex across the face. "How dare you disrespect me in my house?" Eddie asked angrily.

"I'm not trying to be disrespectful, Eddie," Alex said, clutching her face.

"Then what do you call it?"

"I'm just tired, Eddie. I've been up with Eddie Jr. for the past two nights."

"And you think that's supposed to give you a pass from your wifely duties?"

"No, Eddie, I'm not saying that. I just—"

"You just what?" Eddie interrupted. "You want me to go to bed unsatisfied?"

Alex didn't answer. She was tired of having this conversation with Eddie. "I'm tired, Eddie. So I'm going to bed." Alex began to walk toward the bed.

"I don't think so," Eddie said, grabbing Alex and throwing her on the bed. "In my house, I get what I want."

Alex tried to crawl away from Eddie, but he grabbed the back of her neck. He pinned her to the bed and raped her. The closest thing she experienced was when she asked Eddie to stop and he refused when they were at Pendleton. Alex cried silently as she lay face down on the bed, praying it would be over soon. Eddie never raped her before. He had always been aggressive when it came to what he wanted, but she always gave in for fear of what he might do to her. As it turned out, her fears weren't irrational; Eddie was capable of rape. Alex didn't know why she was surprised. Since he put her in the hospital, very few of his actions caught Alex off guard. She was always on her toes expecting a beating and in many cases, expecting to be killed.

She often suspected Eddie might rape her if she ever had enough courage to say no to his advances. But the reality of it was so much worse than anything Alex ever imagined. She felt so helpless and worthless. Every second of the rape made Alex feel dirty. Eddie was supposed to love her. It couldn't be possible for him to do something so brutal, if he loved her. When he was finished, he rolled off her and let out a satisfied sigh.

"I needed that," he said. It sounded like he was smiling. "Go clean yourself off, babe, so we can go to sleep." Alex slowly got up from the bed. She could already feel the soreness in her neck where Eddie's hand pressed into it. As Alex walked toward the bathroom, Eddie called after her. "Let this be a lesson to you," he said. "I get what I want in my house. The next time you disrespect me like that, I won't be so nice about it."

Alex nodded with her back turned to Eddie and closed the bathroom door. She turned on the shower and made it as hot as she could stand it. When she got in, she sat under the stream of water and cried. Alex couldn't believe it. Eddie actually thought raping her was being nice about her alleged disrespect. If the alternative was getting beat up, Alex didn't want to experience either one. Alex grabbed the soap and scrubbed at her skin until it was raw. She felt like she couldn't get clean enough. If she thought the physical abuse was traumatizing, the rape made it all so much worse.

Alex tried to convince herself that it wasn't her fault she was raped, but she had a hard time believing it. If she had just given into Eddie, she wouldn't have been brutalized. If she had just said yes from the beginning, she could have gotten the whole thing over with and went to sleep. Maybe if she hadn't let Eddie drink so much at the restaurant, he wouldn't have raped her. Or maybe if she hadn't worn such a seductive dress, Eddie wouldn't have been so enticed. Alex shuddered to think she had brought the entire situation on herself. She told herself that next time, she would make sure she gave Eddie what he wanted up front.

When the water became cold, Alex got out of the shower. Eddie was asleep when she went back in to the bedroom. She lay down with her back to him and stared at the wall. As she drifted off to sleep, Alex wondered if she could ever find the courage to leave Eddie.

30

*I*t was a beautiful spring day in late March, about two months after her rape, and Alex was exhibiting pregnancy symptoms. She told Eddie she wasn't feeling well, so he took her to the doctor. The doctor conducted a pregnancy test and they learned the results of the test were positive. Eddie was excited to hear the news and Alex forced a smile. She didn't go into hysterics like she did when she learned of her first pregnancy. She wanted to, but thought better of it because Eddie was in the room. She knew this child was conceived during her rape and she hated it. She felt disgusting and wanted to get rid of the baby. But Alex knew she couldn't do it without Eddie finding out. There were still cameras throughout the house and she had no car to drive to a clinic alone. She was stuck having Eddie's baby again.

Alex hoped her current pregnancy would end in the way her first pregnancy ended. In the beginning, she didn't want to have the baby. But as soon as she saw Eddie Jr.'s little face, she couldn't imagine ever letting him go. Maybe she would see this baby's face and feel the same way. Even though she tried to convince herself that everything would be okay, Alex had many doubts. Eddie hadn't raped her when Eddie Jr. was conceived. Although Eddie was a monster even then, she didn't have to deal with the trauma of being raped. Then all of a sudden, Alex remembered something good about having Eddie's baby; she wouldn't get hit. Eddie treated her like royalty when she was carrying Eddie Jr. He gave her anything she wanted and needed and he didn't hit her at all. Alex finally became excited. She would have at least seven abuse-free months to enjoy.

During the ride home, Eddie was discussing baby names. Whenever he would ask her what she thought, Alex would nod and tell him the name sounded good. At this point, she didn't care what the baby's name was. She finally felt like she could breathe for a little while and she wanted to enjoy the first few minutes of it. When they got home, Eddie told Alex that he felt like their current house was too small for a growing family. He said he would go out and buy a new house.

*Cl*ex found out they were moving into a new house in June after Eddie Jr.'s second birthday. She wasn't surprised Eddie hadn't allowed her to house search with him. He rarely included her in the decision making. He would tell Alex about a decision he made and she would have to support it. Eddie bought new furniture for the house and hired movers to move the things they were keeping. Alex finally saw the house for the first time when it was time to move in. Eddie gave her a tour of the entire house.

She couldn't deny it was a beautiful house. It sat near the back of Wilson's Ridge, an affluent neighborhood in northern Gatesville. It was a five-bedroom, 5.5 bathroom brick home with a finished basement and a pool. The front yard was large and beautifully landscaped with a stone walkway leading up to the door. When you walked into the house, there was a study to the right and the living room was to the left. There was a large chef's kitchen and an adjoining dining area just past the living room. The kitchen exited on to a large patio area with a sunroom on the other end of the patio. The master suite was downstairs and the other bedrooms were upstairs. There was a three-car garage, which Alex actually thought was pointless since Eddie wouldn't let her have a car anymore.

When Eddie finished showing her around, he asked Alex what she thought of the house. Overall, Alex liked the house. She did have some concerns about the set up since she was about to have two small children, but she kept her thoughts to herself. She wasn't sure if Eddie would be upset if she said anything negative and she didn't want to test the waters to find out. Alex gave Eddie a smile and told him she loved the house. Eddie seemed happy and gave Alex a hug before leaving to pick up Eddie Jr.

When Alex was alone, she looked closely at the house. There was nothing in it that represented her. Eddie bought the house and furnished it without consulting her. The interior design revolved around Eddie's taste in decor, not hers. The entire layout of the house was convenient for Eddie, but not for her. She didn't like having her bedroom on a different floor when she would have two small children. If they needed her during the night, she would never know and she would worry that they would try to come down the stairs looking for her. She didn't like having a pool because she was afraid that once Eddie Jr. and the new baby were old enough, they would sneak out to the pool and drown. Alex didn't like the living room because anyone who entered it would have to step down into it. Someone would really get hurt if they weren't paying attention.

Overall, Alex felt like the house was too large for a soon-to-be family of four. Most of the time, she would be there by herself. The babies would be in daycare, and then eventually, in school. Eddie spent a lot of time at the office working on cases, so he didn't spend much time at home. Plus, Alex would be responsible for cleaning the entire house. Eddie was leery about having strangers in his house, so she knew there would be no hope in hiring a cleaning service to help her.

Alex suddenly perked up when she looked more intently around the house. There were no cameras anywhere in the house. She assumed Eddie had forgotten to install them or he just hadn't gotten around to it. Alex planned to take full advantage of her freedom until Eddie put the cameras back up. There were several people she wanted to call now that she knew she could speak freely. The first person Alex would call would be Tameka, so she could tell her everything that was really going on with Eddie.

*a*bout a week after the move to Wilson's Ridge, Alex was enjoying life without surveillance. She could talk on the phone during the day and not worry about Eddie monitoring or recording her calls. She could walk outside during the day without having to deal with Eddie's ridiculous time limits. Eddie still wouldn't allow her to go anywhere unsupervised and he hadn't given her cell phone back, but Alex didn't care. She enjoyed the freedom she did have. Even though Alex took pleasure in her daytime freedom, Eddie's nighttime beatings were enough to keep her afraid of taking too many risks. But soon, she would take a big risk. Alex was planning to call Tameka and tell the truth about what she was going through.

Alex took a deep breath as she dialed Tameka's number. She was terrified to make this phone call. She knew Eddie wasn't watching her or monitoring her call, but in the back of her mind she was terrified he would find out about it. Alex's pulse raced faster with each new ring.

"Hello?" Tameka asked cheerfully when she answered.

"Hey, Tameka, this is Alex. How are you?" Alex asked, breathing heavily. She didn't realize she was holding her breath as the phone rang.

"I'm good," Tameka said, slowly. "Why are you breathin' so hard?"

"Because that's what pregnant women do," Alex said. She didn't want to tell Tameka that the real reason she was breathing so hard was because she was afraid Eddie would find out about their conversation. It wouldn't be the right way to ease into such a sensitive topic.

"You're pregnant again?" Tameka asked excitedly. "How far along are you?"

"Almost six months," Alex said.

"Oh my goodness! Why did you wait so long to tell me?"

"I guess it slipped my mind."

"How does pregnancy slip your mind?" Tameka laughed. "You have a constant reminder inside of you."

"Yea, I know. I guess I just have a lot going on."

"Oh, really?" Tameka asked. "Do tell."

"Later. Tell me about what's going on with you first."

"Oh, what's not going on with me? I'm preparing for my graduate internship with Monroe County Schools. Hopefully, they'll like me so much I'll get a job offer when it's over. I'm also datin' this really great guy. I think he might be the one."

"Really? That's wonderful. I'm so happy for you."

"Thank you. I've worked very hard to get this degree. My boyfriend has been really supportive and patient during this entire process, bless his heart. But career counseling is no joke. It's like we have almost double the credit hours of any other graduate program."

"I know. I barely got twenty hours before I left to have Eddie Jr."

"Yea, I know. Why didn't you ever go back? If I remember correctly, you were more passionate about career counseling than I was."

"Eddie thought it would be best if I stayed at home."

"Did he now?" Tameka asked, suspiciously. "And you believed him?"

"I did agree that it would be best for me to be a stay-at-home mom."

"So that's it for you? You stay at home all day doing nothing but cleanin' and takin' care of your child?"

"Is that so bad?"

"Not if that's what you really want to do, but I know better. You've got too much drive to stay at home all day. I remember in undergrad you actually said you would never want to be a stay-at-home mom."

"Well, things change, Tameka. I'm a married woman and I have to do what's best for my family."

"So your family can't support your dreams? You've been Eddie's biggest supporter since day one. It's pretty disturbing to me that he can't do the same for you."

"I'm sure he would, but he's working on his career right now."

"He can't multitask?"

"Come on, Tameka," Alex said. "Cut Eddie some slack please." Alex shook her head in disappointment. The conversation was going in the wrong direction. She was supposed to be telling Tameka about what was going on at home, not defending Eddie.

"All right, I'm not trying to offend you. I'm just concerned, that's all."

"I understand."

"I know you do. I just can't believe you gave up on your dreams for Eddie. It makes it so much worse that he won't even support you in what you want to do. Are you sure this is what you want?"

"I'm not sure anymore, Tameka. I'm really not." Alex took a deep breath and exhaled slowly. She was trying not to cry over the phone.

"What do you mean?" Tameka asked. "Is everything all right at home?'"

Alex took another deep breath. It was now or never. She had to tell someone the truth about what was going on in her marriage. Alex broke down and told Tameka everything she was afraid to tell and everything she couldn't tell due to Eddie's various types of surveillance over the years. She told Tameka about Eddie's control issues and his constant criticisms. She told her about the physical abuse and the trip to the hospital. She also told her about the daily death threats and the rape. When she finished, Tameka was silent.

"Are you still there?" Alex asked nervously.

"Yes," Tameka said, quietly. She sounded like she was crying. "My heart goes out to you, Alex. It really does. I sincerely hoped that I was wrong about Eddie when I told you what I thought about him in undergrad. I know I saw the signs but for your sake, I really hoped my instincts were wrong."

"I know," Alex said. "But you were right. I should've listened to you back then. All the time Eddie was being sweet and caring before we got married was all a ruse. Once we said our 'I dos' it was like he didn't have to pretend anymore. I never knew it was possible for someone to be so cruel."

"I can't even imagine. It's hard to believe that Eddie, of all people, would do this to someone. From the outside lookin' in, he seems almost perfect."

"Yea. He's got everybody fooled."

"Well, Alex, I'm glad you told me what's been going on. Now we have to get you out of there."

"No, Tameka, I can't leave."

"Yes, you can. I'll help you. You can come and live with me in Monroe County. It's pretty far away from Gatesville and I know a couple of cops in this area, so you won't have to worry about Eddie."

"That's not why I'm telling you about my situation, Tameka."

"Then why are you tellin' me?"

"In case something should happen to me, I wanted you to know the truth."

"If something should happen to you? What're you talkin' about?"

"I told you Eddie's been threatening my life. He is getting increasingly volatile and irrational. I'm honestly afraid he is going to kill me."

"Even more reason to leave."

"I'm too terrified to leave."

"Alex, this man is abusin' you, terrorizin' you, and rapin' you. You don't have to live like this."

"I know, but I see no other option. I have no job and very little work experience, so no one will hire me. I have a two-year-old and a baby on the way. How can I leave and bring them with me? I have nothing to offer them. Eddie has this house, a car, and a large bank account. He would take me to court and take my children away from me. I need Eddie."

"No, you don't. You don't need a man who treats you like trash. You already told me that two other people, one of them being Eddie's own mother, have offered to help you get out. If we combine our resources, we can get you and the children out and not have to worry about Eddie."

"If I leave, Eddie will find me. He will kill me and take my children."

"Not if he's in jail."

"No, he can't go to jail!" Alex exclaimed.

"Yea, he can. All you have to do is tell the police what he has done to you."

"Never. He will get out on bail. He will come for me. He will track me down and kill me. He will make it look like someone else did it."

Tameka was silent for a moment. Then she said, "Eddie told you that, didn't he?"

"Told me what?"

"Told you that you couldn't live without him and he would kill you if you left."

"Yes," Alex said, quietly.

"I thought so. None of that is true, Alex. I promise it isn't. There are resources out there for women in your situation. There are safe houses and shelters. Plus, you have your own supportive network of people who are willin' to help you."

"Is that supposed to make me feel better?"

"It should. Some women have no one at all. They have no family or friends because their abuser has cut them off from everyone. And unfortunately, many of them end up getting killed. Domestic violence is a senseless and unnecessary crime, Alex. No one deserves to be beat up or terrorized, especially in their own home. Too many women have died already from this horrifying crime. Don't become a victim of domestic violence. Be a survivor. Let me, or someone else, get you out."

"I can't. I'm sorry."

"Don't apologize to me, Alex. It's your life and your decision. Just promise me something."

"What's that?"

"If you won't leave, then keep a journal and document what's going on with you. That way, if something should happen to you," Tameka said, beginning to choke up, "your death won't be in vain."

"Please, don't cry," Alex pleaded. "Everything is going to fine."

"Not if you stay," Tameka said sobbing. "Just please, make me that promise. Please?"

"I'll try," Alex said slowly. She wasn't too keen about the idea of making a journal. She was afraid Eddie would find it and then her death would be in vain. Eddie would get rid of the evidence and make it seem like someone else murdered her. Alex would have to find the courage to keep a secret journal.

"Good," Tameka said sniffling. "Well, I have to go. Call me and let me know when the new baby is born so I can come and see her."

"We don't know what it's going to be yet."

"Trust me, it'll be a girl. I can feel it."

"Okay," Alex chuckled. "I'll let you know when you can come see the baby."

"Thanks. I love you, Alex. Talk to you later."

"Love you too. Bye."

Alex hung up the phone and sighed. She felt like the conversation went well. She assumed from the beginning Tameka would try to convince her to leave. But Alex was beginning to accept her marriage for what it was—an abusive, codependent relationship. She would no longer think about leaving and she would try her hardest not to upset Eddie. "Till death do us part," Alex said reminiscent of her wedding vows. Since she thought death was the only way out, Alex opted to stay until the end.

The next two years of Alex's marriage proved to be terrifying. Eddie had always been mean, but it seemed like he graduated to being vicious. At times, Alex wondered if he enjoyed tormenting her. There were times when he would berate Alex by calling her horrible names and then he would lift his hand as if he was going to hit her. Instead, he would bring his hand down gently across her cheek as if he was caressing it. Then he would walk away laughing in a manner that always sent chills down Alex's spine. It got to a point where Alex didn't know when she would get hit.

Every time Eddie would lift his arm, Alex would close her eyes and try to shield herself from the blow. Sometimes, she would only feel a gentle touch and other times, she would feel a blow from Eddie's fist. She couldn't predict when Eddie would hit her and when he wouldn't, which intensified Alex's daily fears. Another way he liked to torment Alex was intentional blind sighting. She never saw it coming. Eddie would come home bearing some sort of present for Alex. He would want to take her out for a romantic evening or cook her dinner. He would spend the evening telling her how much he loved her and how beautiful she was. Then he would casually mention something to Alex that he disapproved of. Maybe he felt like the floor needed to be vacuumed or he would want to know why Alex hadn't put the clean dishes up yet. Alex would always apologize profusely and Eddie would always tell her not to worry about it.

The evening would go on and Alex would slowly let her guard down. As soon as Eddie sensed any kind of vulnerability, he would mention his disapproval again. Alex would apologize, but it never worked the second time. How badly Alex got beaten up would depend on what mood Eddie was in. If he wanted to prove he was still in control, he would hit her a few times and call it a night. But if he wanted to really teach Alex a lesson, she would end up going to the hospital.

It was becoming more and more difficult to lie to the ER doctors about all of her injuries. Alex would make up excuses about how she was involved in extreme sports, such as mountain biking and rock climbing. They never believed her and it was probably because she never came into the ER in sweaty, dirty clothes. It would be hard to believe that she got hurt, went home to shower and change, and then went to the hospital for her injury. With all of her trips to the ER, Alex concluded that Eddie was no longer being careful about his abusive nature. He had to know that people would draw conclusions eventually, but he never let up.

It seemed like he was becoming more psychotic and unpredictable. Since Alex had the new baby, whom they named Sarah Nicole James, Eddie had thrown Alex down the stairs, which cracked her ribs, shattered her right knee, and broke her arm. He also bashed her head into the wall, so violently that the gash required ten stitches and she had to deal with the effects of a mild concussion. Hospital staff was surprised she survived such a blow, due to large amounts of blood running from her head. What made matters worse was that Alex believed Eddie did those things to her just because he could. Usually when he would beat her, he would tell her why he was doing it. Those two times he didn't say why; he was just angry for reasons beyond Alex's comprehension.

Alex had to admit she was feeling the effects of Eddie's abuse over the years. She still experienced a slight numbness in her lower lip and chin from the broken jaw she received from her escape attempt. Her eyes seemed to have permanent scarring around them from over a dozen black eyes. Bruises took longer to heal because Eddie hit her in the same places over and over. She had a permanent limp due to her knee injury and it seemed like her arms were constantly in and out of casts. Alex's body ached all the time and she hated it. She couldn't remember what it felt like to not be in pain. She was always waiting for the next bought of pain to be inflicted on her. It had become part of her daily life and it was to the point where she didn't know if she would be able to function normally without it.

After all of the pain Alex endured over the course of their marriage, she was glad she took Tameka's advice to keep a journal. She decided if Eddie did kill her, which seemed like a definite possibility, someone would find the journal and expose Eddie for who he really was. So every time Eddie would hit her, she would type the incident on the computer, date it, then print it for her records. Next, she would take a picture of her injury and print it from their photo printer. When she was finished, she would delete all of the evidence from the computer and camera and put the entry in her special hiding place behind the mirror in her closet. It was a place she knew Eddie would never look since he had his own closet.

Since her conversation with Tameka, Alex had over seventy-five journal entries with pictures hidden in her special hiding place. The journal would have been damning evidence against Eddie if she ever decided to muster up the courage to leave. And that day came sooner than Alex expected.

One Saturday evening, in late August, Alex put Eddie Jr. and Sarah Nicole to bed. It had been a long day for Alex. She spent the entire day running after her toddler age children at the museum and at the park. When she thought they were asleep, Alex went downstairs to clean the kitchen and the living room. It had to be done before Eddie got home because she knew he would be furious if the house wasn't spotless. As she began to walk toward the living room, Alex saw Eddie sitting on the couch waiting for her. He looked angry and Alex knew what was coming.

"Hi, babe," Alex said, forcing a smile. "I didn't hear you come in. How was your day?"

"Why does the living room look like this?" Eddie asked, scanning the living room.

"The kids were playing in here," Alex said, nervously.

"Don't they have a playroom?" Eddie asked as he stood.

"Yes," Alex said quietly.

"I'm sorry, I didn't hear you," Eddie said sarcastically. "What did you say?"

"Yes, Eddie. They have a playroom," Alex said a little louder.

"Then why weren't they in it?"

"It's too far away from the kitchen and I was preparing everyone's dinner. I can watch them better if they're in the living room."

"I've told you time and time again that I don't want them playing in this room, haven't I?" Eddie asked, walking toward Alex.

"Yes," Alex said. "I was going to clean it up, but I—"

"But you, what?" Eddie interrupted. "But you thought you

would clean up before I got here?"

Alex nodded sadly. "Yes," she said. Eddie hit Alex in the stomach and as she bent forward from the pain, Eddie grabbed her face and pushed her to the ground.

"I don't like repeating myself, Alex," Eddie said, standing over her. "You'd think you would've learned that by now, but stupid people don't learn quickly, do they?"

"No," Alex said, gasping for air.

"So since you don't catch on to things quickly, what does that make you, Alex?" Alex didn't say anything. "I said," Eddie said, grabbing a handful of Alex's hair and pulling it, "what does that make you?"

"Stupid," Alex said, wincing from the pain.

"Good girl," Eddie said, patting Alex's cheek as if he were praising a dog for learning a trick. "Stupid. That's exactly what you are. A waste of skin and a waste of life. Stupid people don't deserve to live."

Alex lay on the floor listening to Eddie. She refused to make eye contact for fear of what she might see. The way Eddie was talking made it seem as if he was going to kill her right then.

"Get up," Eddie said, grabbing Alex by the back of the neck and pulling her up. "I'm going out. When I get back, I expect this room to be spotless. If it's not, you will feel my wrath."

Eddie pushed Alex so hard that she tripped over the coffee table and hit her head on one of Eddie Jr.'s toys. Alex lay on the floor crying silently until she heard the door slam. Then she slowly got up and began to gather the toys. When she finished, she made sure the rest of the house was spotless before Eddie came home. She didn't want him to pick a fight over something else. After going through the house, Alex decided she was satisfied and turned in for the night. She made sure she was asleep before Eddie came back home.

34

*T*he next day, Eddie left Alex alone with the children while he went to play golf with some of his colleagues. After the children had lunch, she took them into their playroom and sat with them as they played. She watched Sarah pick up a toy Eddie Jr. just finished playing with. Eddie Jr. became angry and walked over to Sarah. He hit her in the stomach and pushed her down before taking the toy back and walking away. Alex picked up the screaming Sarah and called Eddie Jr. over to her.

"Eddie, why did you do that?" Alex asked, rocking Sarah in her arms. "You know we don't hit."

"She took my toy," Eddie Jr. said clearly still angry.

"You weren't playing with it," Alex said. "So that means she can play with it."

"But it's my toy," Eddie whined.

"It doesn't matter. Say 'you're sorry' to your sister for hitting her."

"Daddy didn't say sorry to you when he hit you," Eddie Jr. said, pleading his case.

"What?" Alex asked, her eyes widening.

"When Daddy hit you, he didn't say sorry. Why do I have to?"

"When did you see Daddy hit me?" Alex asked.

"Last night," Eddie Jr. said. "I heard him talking and I wanted to say good night. I went downstairs to see him and I saw him hit you."

"Oh, honey," Alex said, putting down the now calm Sarah. "You can't always do something because you saw someone else do it."

"What do you mean?" Eddie Jr. asked with a confused look on his face.

"It means just because you saw Daddy do it, doesn't mean it's right."

"If it's not right, then why do you let him do it, Mommy?"

Alex wasn't sure how to answer. She figured the truth would be best. "Because sometimes, Mommy is scared to ask Daddy not to hit her," Alex told him.

"But you told me hitting is bad."

"Yes, it is."

"So does that mean Daddy is bad?"

"It means that Daddy has some bad ways."

"So if Daddy hits you, will he hit me too?"

"I honestly don't know, honey," Alex said, fighting tears.

"Mommy, I don't like getting hit. It hurts."

"Yes it does, sweetie. That's why we don't hit other people."

"So don't let Daddy hit you anymore, okay?"

Alex smiled and nodded. "I'll make a deal with you," she said. "Don't ever hit anybody else ever again and I'll make sure Daddy doesn't hit me ever again. Sound good?"

"Yea," Eddie Jr. said, smiling and hugging Alex.

"Good," Alex said, kissing him on the cheek. "Now go say sorry to your sister."

Alex sat against the wall in the playroom watching her children play. She was mortified by the conversation she just had with Eddie Jr. She couldn't believe he saw Eddie hit her. She never wanted him or Sarah to see her getting beat up. What made the entire situation worse was Eddie Jr. actually thought it was all right to hit another person because he saw his father do it. Alex finally had her wake-up call. She couldn't raise her children in an environment where it was okay to hit other people. Her life and the well-being of her children were at stake. It was time to go.

35

For the next few days, Alex planned her escape. She carefully considered every factor of her exit strategy because she knew if Eddie even suspected she was trying to leave, he would kill her. About a week after her conversation with Eddie Jr., Alex had a plan she was satisfied with. The entire plan would take place over the course of three days. It was risky to take such a long time to get out, but Alex decided to risk it. Eddie had a tendency to come home at odd hours to check on her, so she had to spread it out. Every day for three days, Alex would put garbage bags outside by the garbage can. The bags would be filled with her things and items for the children. She would not put anything out that Eddie would realize was missing until the day she was actually leaving.

Alex decided to use her resources for help. Ms. Esther, the lady who lived across the street from them in their old neighborhood, agreed to help her. She would be the person to pick up the garbage bags every day and take them to her house. On the third day, after Ms. Esther picked up the bags, Alex would call Eddie's mother. She would pick up Alex, pick up the children from daycare, and drive them over to Ms. Esther's house. Ms. Esther would then help them pack all of their things into her car and drive them to Monroe County, where Tameka lived. Monroe County was far enough from Gatesville for Alex to feel safe and Eddie didn't know Tameka lived there, so she thought it was her best option.

Alex wouldn't let Melissa drive her to Monroe, because she didn't want her to feel tempted to tell Eddie where she was staying. It didn't matter how loyal Melissa was to the cause, she was still Eddie's mother.

Ms. Esther, Tameka, and Melissa didn't understand why Alex was taking so long to leave. They told her that since Eddie was so volatile and unpredictable, she should leave everything behind and disappear. But Alex couldn't do that. She wanted to be able to start her new life with something. She felt bad enough getting others involved in her situation, and she didn't want them to have to buy new clothes for her and the children in addition to all the help they were already giving her.

Before Alex put her plan into effect, she went to the secret place where her journal was hidden. She glued the pictures to its corresponding entry and bound it together. Then she went into Eddie's study and took a large envelope, a few stamps, and a piece of paper. She sat down at his desk and began to write.

Dear Tameka,

As you know from our last conversation, I am leaving Eddie and coming to stay with you until I get on my feet. I had gotten to the point in my relationship where I was going to accept what was being done to me. I felt like I needed Eddie and that there was no way out. And much to my chagrin, I was willing to die here. That was until I saw Eddie Jr. hitting Sarah. He actually thought it was all right to hit her because he saw Eddie do it to me. So that was my wake up call. I won't be respon-

sible for raising a monster. Even though I am finally making an attempt to leave, I find myself almost paralyzed with fear. I am afraid that Eddie will find out and kill me. Remember, I told you about him repeating the wedding vow to me after our wedding ceremony? "Till death do us part, Alex. Remember that." That's what he said to me. He has also threatened my life on almost a daily basis and I know, if caught, he is crazy enough to kill me. At one point, I was afraid to leave because of what people would think about me. No one would ever believe that Eddie was an abuser. Most people believe he's a saint. They can't see past his intelligence, charm, and good looks to see the monster that he really is. Today is Tuesday and I am supposed to be seeing you on Friday. If I don't make it to you, assume the worst, but don't let me die in vain. My journal is included with this letter. Publish it and show the world what was really going on. I want everyone to know the truth about Eddie James. I'm going to wrap up this letter now, but I just want you to know how much I love you and cherish our friendship. You know, just in case...Send up a prayer for me and expect to see me later.

Love, Alexandria ~~James~~ Stamford

Alex smiled when she finished the letter. She had crossed out "James" and put her maiden name in its place. She would no longer be a slave to that name or a victim to its owner. Alex slid the journal into the envelope and put the letter on top. After she addressed it, she took it outside just as the mailman was pulling up to her mailbox. She handed the package to him. Alex was glad she planned her letter writing at that particular time. She knew better than to have something like that sitting in the mailbox. Eddie wouldn't allow her to touch the mailbox, let alone, get the mail. He liked to go through it and see what was there. It was his way of making sure Alex wasn't plotting against him or communicating with someone he didn't want her to communicate with. Alex walked into the house and sat on the couch. She was terrified of what had to happen in the next few days.

It was such a big risk to leave over an extended period of time, especially when she was dealing with someone as obsessive as Eddie. He made sure everything was in a certain place. It seemed to Alex that he always knew when something had been moved; even if it was just a couple of inches. Eddie was paranoid and irrational. He would easily jump to conclusions about something he felt like Alex had done. He accused her of flirting with other men and having countless affairs. He accused her of plotting against him by turning his children against him. He would also accuse her of secretly informing people that he was abusive. For every one of his accusations, Alex would get beat up. If Eddie even got a hint that Alex was trying to leave, her fate would be sealed. For the next few days, Alex would have to be more obsessive and more paranoid than Eddie if she wanted to prevent him from discovering her plan. Having spent years around Eddie's psychotic behavior, Alex believed she could do it.

36

*W*ednesday was Alex's first day of putting out the clothes for Ms. Esther to pick up. It went more smoothly than she anticipated. Alex put three trash bags by the garbage can around noon and they were gone about thirty minutes later. Thursday went as smoothly as Wednesday, but Alex was becoming more and more nervous. She just had one more day to be in the same house with Eddie. From what Alex could tell, he was oblivious to what she was doing.

When Thursday night came, Alex had the hardest time getting to sleep. She was beginning to second-guess her decision to leave. She knew Eddie had the money to hire a private detective to find her if he wanted, and he already told her many times that the only way out was death. Alex shuddered when she thought about what Eddie would do to her if he found out she was trying to leave. She knew what he did to her when she wasn't trying to escape, so she figured her death would be brutal as well. Alex took a deep breath in order to calm her nerves. She had gotten this far in her escape attempt and it was senseless to back out now. Friday would be the final day of her plan. She would finally leave Eddie and the moment couldn't come quickly enough.

On Friday morning, Alex got up early as usual to help everyone prepare for their day. She woke up the children and got them into the bathroom to wash them up and get them dressed. She went down to the kitchen and made everyone breakfast. While they ate, she made sure everyone had what they would need to go to their respective locations. When the children finished eating, Eddie walked into the kitchen. He kissed the children on their foreheads and picked up a glass of orange juice.

"Where's my briefcase?" he asked Alex, after taking a sip of juice.

"In your study," Alex said, offering him some eggs.

"You moved it?" Eddie asked coldly.

"Yes. The children were up early this morning, and I didn't want them playing with it."

"Okay," he said. "It's going to be a long day today, so I probably won't be home for dinner."

"Okay, what would you like me to make?"

"Spaghetti Bolognese."

"Garlic bread?"

"Yea. And a salad."

"Okay, I will make you a plate and store it for you."

"Good girl," Eddie said, kissing Alex on the forehead. "Sarah, Eddie, let's go."

Having conversations like that was one of the many reasons Alex wanted to leave Eddie. He just had to feel powerful and in control of everything. Even when he was working late, she still had to cook. It didn't matter whether or not he was going to eat it; he just wanted it done. If he came home and there was no cooked food waiting for him, he would have a fit that usually ended with Alex receiving some kind of injury. His controlling nature had worn Alex out. She was glad to be leaving. Eddie Jr. grabbed his bag from Alex and sprinted toward the door. Eddie followed Eddie Jr., yelling at him to slow down, while Sarah slowly pulled up the rear. As they headed out the door, the children said goodbye to Alex. When Alex was sure they were gone, she began to prepare for her final day under Eddie's rule.

She went into the children's rooms and packed the things that Eddie would notice were missing. She packed more of her clothing and other miscellaneous items. Alex wanted to take some of the money Eddie had hidden in his special hiding place, but thought better of it. She refused to give Eddie a reason to put a warrant out on her for stealing. Alex knew he would do something like that in order to find her. When Alex finished packing, she placed the bags outside by the garbage cans and called Ms. Esther to come pick them up.

Alex was more nervous than she was the last couple of days and she wasn't sure why. She was only about an hour away from freedom and Eddie wouldn't be home all day. She was panicking for nothing. Alex stared at the window until she saw Ms. Esther load the bags into her car and pull off. Alex had to admit, she was impressed by Ms. Esther. She had amazing strength for a woman her age, and she came and picked up the bags so nonchalantly that Alex could have sworn she had been rescuing abuse victims for years. *It's almost over,* Alex thought still trying to calm her nerves. Talking to herself wasn't helping Alex calm down so she decided to take a shower.

When she got out, she threw on the clothes she was going to wear to Tameka's house. Then she went downstairs and sat on the sofa. As she picked up the phone to call Melissa, she had an eerie feeling. Alex decided to shake it off and dialed the number.

"Hello?" Melissa answered.

"Hey, it's me. I'm ready," Alex said.

"On my way," Melissa said and they both hung up. Alex entwined her fingers on her lap as she waited for Melissa. She hadn't been waiting long when she learned why she had gotten the eerie feeling.

"What're you ready for, Alex?" came Eddie's voice from behind her.

Alex didn't move. She was paralyzed with fear. She was hoping that hearing Eddie's voice was a figment of her imagination. "I said 'what're you ready for?'" Eddie repeated.

Alex wasn't imagining anything. Eddie was in the house and he was somewhere behind her.

"Eddie, when did you get back?" Alex asked, trying to deflect the question. She still refused to look behind her.

"Not important," Eddie said. "And I'm still waiting on an answer."

"Your mom wanted to take me shopping, so she's coming to pick me up," Alex said, hoping Eddie would buy it.

"You've always been a horrible liar, Alex," Eddie said, chuckling in his usual sadistic manner. Alex finally turned around to look at Eddie. What she saw made her sick to her stomach. Eddie was holding a gun in his hand and he looked like he was two seconds away from having a meltdown. His tie was hanging loosely around his neck and his shirt wasn't tucked in. His eyes darted around the room wildly and his breaths were short and erratic. "Why don't you tell me the truth this time, Alex," Eddie said, not moving.

"Eddie, put the gun down," Alex said, putting her hands out in front of her as she stood.

"You want me to put the gun down, Alex? What about what I want?" he asked, pointing it at Alex.

"Eddie, we can talk about this. Just put the gun down," Alex pleaded.

"Not until you tell me what I want to know," Eddie said, tears streaming down his cheeks. "What're you ready for? Ready to leave me?"

"No," Alex answered before she even thought about it.

Eddie shook his head. "You're still lying to me. I came back here to see you for lunch because one of my meetings got cancelled. When I pull around the corner, I see some woman picking up bags from around our trash can and driving away. I come into the house to see if you know anything about it and I feel like something's off. I go in our room to find you and I see most of the things in your closet gone. Things from the kids' rooms- gone. So then I put the two events together and realized you planned this. You're trying to leave me, aren't you, Alex?"

Alex knew she couldn't lie so she said, "Yes."

"And my kids? You're taking them too?"

"Yes," Alex said quietly.

Eddie lowered the gun and shook his head. "I can't believe this," he said, wiping his eyes with his free hand. "I've given you everything and this is how you repay me? You try to leave me and take my kids from me? How could you do this to me?"

"I can't take the abuse anymore," Alex said, trying not to cry.

"So this is it then? You're just going to leave?"

"I have to Eddie," Alex said, eyeing the gun.

"I don't think so," Eddie said, pointing the gun at Alex again. "I knew I wanted to be with you since the day I met you. I can't live without you, Alex. I just can't. Please don't leave me, Alex," Eddie pleaded.

"I can't stay, Eddie."

"But I can change, I promise. What do you want? I'll give you anything you want. Do you want a bigger house? I can buy that for you. A new wardrobe? Let's go and get it now. A car? More vacations? What can I do? Please tell me what I can do and I will do it."

"You can let me go," Alex said.

"So that's it then?" Eddie asked angrily. "You're going to be a coward and leave me? You'll never make it without me. You'll never find a job. You'll never be able to buy a house and you'll never meet a man who can love you like I do."

"I'm willing to take that chance."

"You're not taking my kids away from me, Alex," Eddie said, walking over to Alex and grabbing her arm.

"You can't change my mind, I'm leaving and they're coming with me," Alex said. She was still mindful of the gun as she tried to twist her arm out of his grip.

Eddie pushed Alex to the floor and sat down on the bottom stair. He buried his head in his free hand and cried. Alex almost felt sorry for him, but she knew his tears weren't sincere. She assumed they were part of his manipulative plan to get her to stay. Alex slowly got up and inched toward the door as Eddie cried. She didn't want to be in the room when Eddie realized his plan wasn't working.

"Don't move!" Eddie yelled, pointing his gun at Alex. "You can't do this to me, Alex. You just can't. You can't leave me. Please, tell me you won't leave me."

"I can't," Alex said.

Eddie let out a heavy sigh and shook his head. After wiping the tears from his eyes, he said, "I can't live without you, Alex, and I won't. I'm sorry but I can't let you live anymore."

"Eddie, no!" Alex screamed as she backed away from him.

"I'm sorry," Eddie said as he shot Alex in the chest.

Alex fell on the floor gasping for breath. She could feel the life draining out of her as she stared at the door. Eddie finally did it. He finally made good on his promise. She was almost free. She had almost made it out. But now she was dying. As Alex lay on the floor, she could feel her heart slowing down. As she became weaker, she fought to keep her eyes open but she couldn't. Blood was gushing from her chest and Alex was beginning to feel cold. Soon she was delirious, but she thought she could still hear Eddie crying hysterically. Before Alex completely lost consciousness, she heard another gunshot. She wanted to call Eddie's name, but she was too weak to do it. As Alex lay in the silence dying, she silently prayed that someone would find her before it was too late. When she finished her prayer, she lost consciousness.

When Alex opened her eyes again, she was lying in the hospital. The last time she woke up in the hospital, Eddie had almost beaten her to death. Everyone who knew about her injuries said it was a miracle that she even survived. Alex often felt as if she wouldn't get another chance to cheat death if Eddie decided he wanted her dead. But she had always been too afraid to leave. Eddie spent the bulk of their six-year marriage tormenting her. He was cruel to her; he would beat her senseless; he raped her; and he controlled everything she did. After all of that, Alex wasn't sure what to expect next.

Alex looked around the room and saw many of the people she knew. She saw her mother, her grandfather, Tameka, and Eddie's parents. Alex acknowledged their presence and looked around the room. Eddie wasn't there and neither were her children. Alex tried to sit up, but her mother put her hand on her shoulder.

"Relax, sweetie," she said. "You've been through a lot."

"Eddie Jr. and Sarah. Where are they?" Alex asked frantically.

"They're with George," Alex's mother said. "We didn't want them to see you like this."

"And Eddie…where is he?" Alex asked slowly.

"Oh honey," Alex's mother said, putting her hand on Alex's cheek and looking at Melissa.

"He killed himself," Melissa said with tears streaming down her face.

"So the gunshot I heard after he shot me, it was real?" Melissa nodded her head and cried as Sebastian held her in his arms. "I can't believe it," Alex said, beginning to cry herself.

"Well, I do and good riddance," Alex's grandfather said.

"Dad," Alex's mom snapped.

"I'm just saying, Mickey. The boy was abusing her. This is the second time she almost died."

"Why don't you go get the doctor and relieve George," Michaela said. "And do a better job of comforting the children than you did in here. After all, it was their father who just died." Alex's grandfather huffed and exited the room. "I'm sorry about him," Michaela said to Eddie's parents. "He can be a little high strong."

"I understand," Melissa said. "After all, Eddie is the one that did this to her and I feel terrible about it. We raised him to be so much better than this."

"I'm sure you tried your best. I just wish it could have ended differently," Michaela said solemnly.

"Knock, knock," Dr. Fields said as she entered the room with George. "Well, well, well, Mrs. James, I'm honestly glad to say that it's good to see you again."

"How is it good?" Alex asked. "I'm in the hospital."

"You could've been in the morgue. That's why I'm saying it's good to see you."

"Was the wound really that bad?"

"Yes. The bullet penetrated about an inch away from your heart and collapsed a lung. You lost a lot of blood and if your mother-in-law hadn't found you when she did, you wouldn't have even made it to the operating table."

"So you're the person who found me?" Alex asked Melissa.

She nodded and said, "Yes. I heard a gunshot when I pulled up to your house. I thought Eddie had shot you. I ran in the house and I saw you lying near the door, chest bleeding and not breathing. Then I saw him lying on the floor near the stairs with his entire head bloody and gory. It looked like he'd shot himself in the head. I thought both of you were dead. But when the para- medics got there, they were able to get you breathing. But it was too late for—" Melissa couldn't finish her statement. She began to cry again.

"I'm really sorry for your loss, Mr. and Mrs. James," Dr. Fields said. "It's always hard losing someone you love." Melissa nodded and continued to cry. "So Alex," Dr. Fields said, getting back to Alex, "We were able to remove the bullet successfully and I am optimistic about your recovery. I do want to keep you here for a couple more days for observation and then we'll turn you loose."

"Okay," Alex said. "What kind of condition is my house in?"

"I don't know, Alex," Dr. Fields said.

"No one has cleaned it up yet," Sebastian said.

"We'll make sure it's cleaned before you and the kids get there,"George said.

"Thanks, Uncle George," Alex said.

"If you need anything or if you have any concerns about your condition, please page me," Dr. Fields said, giving Alex her card.

"I do have one request," Alex said, not making eye contact.

"What's that?" Dr. Fields asked.

"Can I see Eddie?" she asked.

"Sure," Dr. Fields said. "I'll send him in when I leave."

"No, not Eddie Jr.," Alex said. "Eddie, my husband."

"We've already had him moved to the funeral home," Sebastian said. "Plus, I don't think you would want to see him. His face is pretty messed up."

"I don't care. I need to see him," Alex insisted.

Sebastian sighed. "When you get out of here, I'll take you to see him."

"Thanks," Alex said.

"Page me if you need anything, Alex and I'll be back to check on you later," Dr. Fields said, before she left.

Alex stared at the ceiling as she tried to make sense of everything that happened over the past few days. She executed her plan to leave Eddie, and got caught on her last day. Eddie found out and intended to kill her when she told him she wouldn't stay. Now she was lying in the hospital after having a bullet removed from her chest. She was alive but her husband was dead.

Alex didn't know how to feel. She couldn't deny that she loved Eddie. Her love for him was one of the reasons she stayed in the marriage for so long; that, and her fear of Eddie tracking her down and killing her after she left. But Alex was also experiencing another emotion other than grief; she felt relief. She wouldn't have to live in fear anymore. She wouldn't have to constantly look over her shoulder and live her life as her husband's punching bag.

"Till death do us part, Alex. Remember that." Eddie's words still rang in Alex's head. She had to give Eddie some credit. He did make good on his promise that only death would separate them. Although, Alex doubted his words meant that he would be the one dying.

When Alex was feeling up to it, she finally saw her children. She could tell they were distraught over the news of their father's death. Eddie Jr. was four and Sarah was almost two; there was no way they were able to understand why their father wouldn't be coming home again. Alex's heart broke as she tried to explain it to them in a way they would understand, which only made them more confused and miserable. Alex held them in her arms and promised them that it would get better. She told them they would heal together.

After Alex got out of the hospital, Sebastian took her to see Eddie. He warned her that Eddie was in bad shape, but Alex wasn't concerned about that. She assumed Eddie would look bad after she was told he shot himself in the head. Her primary reason for wanting to see Eddie in his coffin was to confirm in her mind that he was really gone. Anyone who heard her say she wanted to make sure Eddie was dead would think she was pretty cold-hearted. But no one knew what she had really been through with that man, and Alex knew she wouldn't be able to heal and move on if she didn't see him.

Alex cried as she stared at Eddie's lifeless body in the coffin. She cried tears of grief for her children who couldn't understand the magnitude of what was going on. She also cried in relief for herself. It was finally over. She was free. Alex put a hand on her lips, then placed it on Eddie's distorted cheek. She thanked Sebastian for letting her see him and they left the funeral home. Alex didn't attend Eddie's funeral. As far as she was concerned, she already said her good-byes when she saw him lying in his casket. Alex knew her healing would take time. But she had no idea, what her healing would actually feel like. Soon after Eddie's death, Alex began to have night terrors. They were so vivid and felt so real that she could have sworn Eddie was haunting her from his grave. It seemed she wasn't free from Eddie James after all.

·

AFTERWORD

I wrote *The Truth About Eddie James* as a cautionary tale for women everywhere. Intimate Partner Violence (also known as domestic violence) can affect anyone; your background, race, and financial situation does not exclude you. In fact, the CDC calls Intimate Partner Violence a serious, public health issue that affects millions of people a year. Speak out against relationship violence. Let's end the cycle of abuse.

If you, or someone you know, needs help getting out of a violent relationship, contact the National Domestic Violence Hotline. They have 24/7 phone support and varying hours for Live Chat. Representatives can assist you with getting the help that you need:

National Domestic Violence Hotline
www.thehotline.org
1-800-799-SAFE (7233)
1-800-787-3224 (toll free)

ABOUT THE AUTHOR

Jessica Glaspie is an emerging author in women's fiction and nonfiction. Her blog, Relationship Recovery, focuses on encouraging women to create successful relationships by healing from past hurts and growing closer to God. This is Jessica's first book.

For your weekly dose of encouragement and information about upcoming book releases, visit:

www.YourRelationshipRecovery.com

www.ingramcontent.com/pod-product-compliance
Lightning Source LLC
Chambersburg PA
CBHW050358030726
47503CB00006B/1921